Newfound Amazing Adventure

Newfound Amazing Adventure

Compiled and Edited by
Dr. Susmita Gupta

Written by
26 Amazing Student Authors

Anecdote

Anecdote
Publishing House
For the love of quality reading!

Anecdote Publishing House
E-35-A, E Block, Gali No. 2 Ganesh Nagar,
Pandav Nagar Complex Delhi-110092

Published by Anecdote Publishing House

First Edition 2023
Second Reprint 2024

ISBN 978-81-963155-0-4

MRP ₹ 295

Book Promoted and Marketed by Champ Readers Pvt. Ltd.

Cover and Layout by Aaush Kumar
Printed by Thomson Press (India) Ltd, New Delhi

CONTENTS

ACKNOWLEDGMENTS

I am eternally grateful to all the talented writers who contributed to the completion of this book with their splendid craft of writing without whom this 'Newfound' wouldn't have been discovered. Cheers to my readers for reading my books and encouraging me to write more. Writing a book is a surreal process and the successful completion of this book was possible only because of the tremendous support of the entire team of DWPS (Delhi World Public School – Noida Extension) and the respected Principal, together with the teachers and the entire Authority who blessed me with such amazingly talented student writers. It's very kind of you all!

Forever indebted to the blessings of the almighty without which I wouldn't have succeeded so far. Thanks a million!

To my family and the closed ones; I am overwhelmed in all humbleness and gratefulness to acknowledge my depth well above the level of simplicity and into something concrete. Any attempt at any level can't be satisfactorily complete without your support and guidance. Your encouragement and support when the time got turbulent are much appreciated and duly noted. Much love to all!

The completion of this book would not have been possible without the unwavering dedication and support of my publishing team at Anecdote Publishing House. I would like to express my deepest gratitude for their unwavering cooperation throughout the entire process. I would also like to thank all those who have contributed to this book, both known and unknown. Your efforts have not gone unnoticed and I credit each and every one of you for your valuable contributions. From the bottom of my heart, thank you!

INTRODUCTION

One day, as I was scrolling through my inbox, a letter inviting me to speak to the students at Delhi World Public School - Noida Extension about my literary journey popped up. I was filled with awe when I actually faced them and discovered this Newfound talent of writing of such cute little souls.

I feel incredibly fortunate to have been a part of that event, and it was then that I decided to highlight their love of writing by establishing them as authors. They have given me their craft of writing and I have got a chance to be their compiler of beautiful tales. I also consider myself extremely fortunate to be in a position to share with the world every fantasy and imagination the students have shared through their writing. With due permission from the school authority and parents of the student authors "Newfound – Amazing Adventure" was born.

With their fantastical tales, the young storytellers in this book will shuttle you to a different world, and some of their tales will even give you goosebumps. The stories in this book were selected from among the hundreds of submissions we received. As a product of the imagination, fiction has inherent limitations to what we can conceive. However, I am confident that these tales will captivate and entertain you as much as they did me, and that they will inspire you in the same way they inspired me.

Dr. Susmita Gupta

Newfound Amazing Adventure

Chapter 1

The Land of the Rainbow

Reyansh Nath Mukherjee

In a coastal orphanage in Miami, Florida, there lived a boy named John. He was an orphan and had four close friends in the orphanage: Harry, Joseph, Rosetta, and Daniel. John was given the responsibility of maintaining the garden by Mr. Smith, the man in charge of the orphanage.

One day, while tending to the pumpkin plants, John accidentally overwatered one of them. Reflecting on his mistake, he thought to himself, "I must be more careful with how much water I give the plants. Tomorrow, I'll water them a little less." With this in mind, John returned inside, determined to be more attentive in his gardening duties.

The pumpkin grew bigger and bigger. Next day, John saw that the pumpkin had grown to a gigantic size. He went inside and called out to his friends, "Hey! Come with me to the garden! I have something interesting to show you." His friends followed him to the garden. Rosetta, looking at the pumpkin, suggested, "Let's lift this pumpkin and use it as a boat. We will go on an adventure!" So, the five friends lifted the pumpkin and gently let it down on the sea. Then Harry, John, Joseph, and Rosetta climbed up the pumpkin. Since Daniel was an expert climber, he pushed the pumpkin and quickly climbed up.

The pumpkin set sail. They travelled for hours until darkness settled over them. Harry had a knife which he used to cut a hole in the pumpkin for them to sleep in. Next day, they climbed out of the hole and saw that they had reached an island. Everything on the island was bathed in the seven colours of the rainbow – the bushes, the grass, the trees, the buildings, and the vehicles. The friends exclaimed, "Whoa!"

They walked on and reached a city. They were shocked to see that even the people had rainbow-coloured skin! Joseph asked one of them, "What is this place? Why is everything and everyone here rainbow–coloured?" The man replied, "The name of this country is Beaurenbourge. Nobody except the king knows why everything is rainbow coloured. The king has made a rule that only a person who isn't rainbow–coloured can ask him this question. So, if you follow me, I will lead you to him." The five friends followed the man. On the way, he told them that his name was Charles.

After a few minutes' walk, they reached the king's giant palace. Seeing the five friends and Charles, one of the guards asked them, "What is your purpose for coming here?" Charles replied, "These five foreigners wish to ask the king a question."

The other guard said to the five friends, "Please follow me inside." They did so and reached the king. The guard bowed in front of the king and said, "Your Majesty, these people wish to ask you something." Then he left the room.

Daniel asked, "Your Majesty, why does every single thing and person here have the seven colours of the rainbow?" The king replied, "Since you are not rainbow–coloured, I will tell you the answer to your question.

Many centuries ago, this place was built by the Nasinaks. However, all of them died when a highly contagious disease spread across them. All the materials were naturally rainbow–coloured, due to which everything they built contained the seven colours. These (he pointed towards the benches, buildings, vehicles, bushes, and trees outside the window) are those same things that have been maintained so well that they look like they have been built recently. Since all the Nasinaks also were rainbow–coloured and we are their last descendants, all the people here bear the same colours. Any more questions?" "No, Your Majesty. Thank you for all the information. We will leave now." replied Harry. The king added in a whisper,

"Promise me that you will not tell anyone the story." They nodded and left the palace.

Charles was waiting for them outside, eager to know what the king might have told them. As soon as he saw them, he asked, "How'd it go? Did he answer your question? Can you tell me why we have rainbow-coloured skin?" John answered, "It went well. His Majesty did answer our question, but he forbade us to disclose it to anyone else." Hearing this, Charles walked away sadly.

Rosetta asked, "What do we do now?" "We live here for four days, starting from today, and set sail for the orphanage." replied Joseph.

At the orphanage, Harry had learnt to build houses from wood. He gave the others directions and within a few hours, the five friends had built a decent wooden house for themselves. They borrowed a blanket from Charles to sleep on. It was large enough for the five of them. Charles introduced them to a woman named Jennie who agreed to provide them with food for the next four days. They visited a rainbow–coloured river. They saw that many people were bathing in it. So, to have fun, they too, dived into it.

They splashed around in the river for a while and then returned home. Next, they ate lunch and took a short nap.

When they woke up in the evening, John suggested, "Let's go on an evening stroll." The others agreed and they started walking on the pavement.

Suddenly, they came upon an abandoned ball. Harry said, "Let's go back home and play baseball using this ball and a piece of log that we found earlier. The area behind our house is perfect for playing the sport." His friends agreed and they played till half past nine, after which they had dinner and slept.

They made this a daily routine.

On the last day, after eating breakfast, they went to Charles's house. He called his two kids to play with them. They played a game in which John, Harry, and Joseph pretended to be enemies and Rosetta, Daniel and the kids had to pretend–fight them and drive them away. They had a lot of fun. During lunchtime, the friends bade farewell to Charles and his children and went to Jennie to say goodbye to her.

Then they set sail on their pumpkin again.

Chapter 2

Gaur City 2 – A New Experience

Espen Ooyevaar

Leaning over to get a better view, I craned my neck until it bumped into the seat in front of me. Out the dark window yellow lights shone through the clouds, at first tiny but getting bigger and bigger all the time. It was my first view of the country that would be my home for the next year. As we dipped down through the haze, streets began to appear, and houses spread out below me. This memory will always have a place in my mind. It was the first time that the anticipation and excitement that had been building for months had a physical manifestation. My dream was becoming a reality.

Fourteen hours ago, my fellow YES/AFS Abroad students and I had boarded our flight, feeling both nervous and excited. However, as I gazed out of the airplane window and saw India for the first time, I was overcome by a surge of emotions I had never experienced before. My excitement was tempered by apprehension as a myriad of questions flooded my mind: How will I cope with being away from my family for nine months?

Will I be able to adapt to a new culture? What will life be like in India?

For the next five days, me and three other high schoolers from the US went through an orientation about our lives for the next nine months. In between language classes, we watched presentations about everything from Delhi's climate to life in a joint family. Wandering around the hotel, we practiced our Hindi by attempting to have conversations with the hotel staff. We might've had trouble understanding each other, but it was exhilarating to take the first step into a new language, and therefore a new culture.

We spent a lot of time during that orientation staring out the window of our hotel wondering how we would fit in with the world outside. Below the hotel, stretched Jaipur Road right as it entered the National Capital Territory of Delhi. At night, the lines for the toll booth at that junction would snake further and further until the entire highway was a sea of red and white lights. I couldn't wait to be a part of the traffic jam.

Following the orientation, my host father arrived to take me home. As we drove down the same highway I had been gazing at for the past five days, I couldn't help but feel a sense of anticipation. After arriving at the apartment building, we rode the elevator up to the fourteenth floor, where I was finally introduced to my new family.

The question lurking in the back of my mind as the plane landed at Indira Gandhi Airport was one that I didn't let myself come face to face with until I'd settled into my host family's house: what if I fail? There wasn't one specific thing that could go "wrong", but that was the problem. There seemed to be so many unknowns, unknowns that could throw off the course of my exchange. I thought of stories from alumni of my program who had completed their exchange. They had made their share of blunders. But when they knew they had messed up, they kept going. I decided to learn from their perseverance.

In November, the whole extended family gathered in Gurgaon for Chhath Puja. For two days, we supported Naniji as she performed the Puja. Those two days were full of learning about one of Bihar's biggest festivals. We ate Prasad fruit and Thekua which Naniji had offered in prayer at sunrise. My favorite part of the festival was spending time with my host relatives, playing Ludo and hopscotch with cousins and watching India play in the T20 Cricket World Cup with the whole family.

Yesterday marked four months of living in India. It feels like I've been here for a day and a year at the same time. In those four months I've learned more than I can comprehend right now. I think it'll take a couple of years to sink in just how incredible this experience was. One of my biggest takeaways from my time here so far is the power language has, to break down barriers between people. I can attribute any success I've had fitting into my community to the Hindi I've learned so far. Speaking the same language immediately puts me and the person I'm speaking to in the same field of communication. It's a tool I've used more and more as I've gotten comfortable speaking Hindi. Reflecting on the last four months, I can see how far I've come. I can trace the growth of my cultural understanding as I celebrated Navratri, Diwali, and Chhath Puja. It's not an exaggeration to say that I still learn more every day. Looking ahead to the next four months, I have so much more to learn from this abundant country, and I can't wait.

Chapter 3

LILY AND HER FAIRY JOURNEY

Bhoovi Soni

Once upon a time, there was a girl named Lily. She was five and had pretty brown eyes, golden hair, that had a silky texture and she always wore a wonderful outfit. Adorable Lily also had a cute smile. Her dream was to be a fairy of a flower garden one day.

Through the years she had a habit of plucking flowers whenever she came across some beautiful ones. When she was 15 years old, she was poisoned by a witch, who did not want Lily to become a fairy. The poison was rapidly coursing through Lily's body, leaving her struggling for breath. Witnessing this, her parents were overcome with worry, and her mother began to weep uncontrollably.Lily's father came up with the idea to take Lily to the fairy, Amelia. Amelia's castle was a huge one. It had four rooms, drawing, dining, kitchen, and a big bedroom that was also the centre of attraction.

The main room had a piano in the middle, towards the corner there was a couch, television and a round shaped bed. Near the window, stood Amelia. Lily's parents were awestruck to see the beauty that Amelia was blessed with. She had blue eyes, wore a pink gown and had a yellow wand in her hand. Lily's parents told her all that had happened. The fairy felt sorry for poor Lily. She gave them a magic potion of healing. Lily's mother sprinkled the potion on Lily's body and soon she regained consciousness. The three of them were elated to see Lily all hale and hearty. Her parents requested fairy Amelia, to keep Lily with her and educate, guide and teach her how to be a good fairy.

Lily's journey to fulfil her dream began from then on. For the next five years she was taken care of by Amelia like her own child. Right from the moment Lily opened her eyes in the morning till the minute she slept, she was like a shadow to Amelia. She learnt how to face the different challenges and how to help people in times of need. All the traits of a good fairy were taught to her and her inner beauty outshined as time passed. She also made many new fairy friends whose company taught Lily to live through thick and thin.

After a span of five long years, it was time for Lily to go back home to her parents. With a heavy heart she bid goodbye to her fairy friends and walked along with Amelia. All the way, Lily's eyes had tears into them as she didn't want to leave her. She recalled the best moments that she had at the fairy's house. Soon she reached her parents place where her mother welcomed her and hugged her tightly. The apple of her eye was finally home. Lily's father was glad to see both of them and the way his daughter had grown up with all the good values. She followed the path of selflessness and believed in helping each other in times of need. Thus, she too led the life of a fairy giving unconditional love to others and got love in return.

Moral: Always work hard to fulfil your dreams and then nothing can stop you.

Chapter 4

THE LAST DREAM

Arnav Kukreja

March 26, 1927. A day forever etched in the memories of Jack and his friends, for the adventures and terrors they faced. It all began on March 24th, when Jack received a letter from his childhood friend, Steve. Steve informed him of a new order from their boss, Peter, to explore a new cave in Florida and extract valuable ores and minerals. Little did they know that Peter was a greedy man who would put his workers' lives at risk for the sake of his own greed. The most horrifying detail about the cave was that anyone who had ventured into it never returned, earning it the ominous nickname, "The Death Cave."

Jack sent a letter to his other colleagues and decided to explore the cave on the 26th of March. It didn't take much for them to reach Florida because all of them lived in Georgia. When they reached the cave, they saw a board that was fully red and couldn't notice what was written on it. As they went closer, they realised that the board was fully red not because of any type of paint but because of blood. They didn't realise that the start of their journey to explore would start like this. Andrew (a colleague of jack) removed the blood on the board with some water and read the sign, their eyes widened as they read the sign. The sign had a message from a previous explorer James Charles and he wrote with his blood that "DON'T, JUST DON'T ENTER". They all panicked and Jack and Andrew decided to cancel this project, but Steve made them all agree to go on with the mission because he knew their boss would kill them all if they abort the mission. Finally, they all decided to enter the cave.

The cave had a narrow opening, Jack decided to enter the cave first with his bag-pack having all the necessary equipment, firstly he couldn't see anything because of the darkness and later switched on his torch and the first thing he saw was a 'ripped off head' hanging on the wall and screamed, after listening to Jack's scream Steve, Andrew and Lana entered the cave one by one and saw Jack trembling with fear. They asked Steve what's the problem and he pointed toward the hanging head. They all started to scream and just sat at the moment to relax for a bit, they decided to ignore the hanging face but as they were passing by, Lana saw a badge just below the head to identify who was the person, and realised it was the badge of the same person who had written the sign on the board

(James Charles). As they were walking down the cave, their journey started getting worse. They saw so much blood and bodies all over the cave and couldn't guess why the others died.

Further away they saw a rope going down to the bottom of the cave but decided not to go to the bottom so early, as they were walking in the cave Lana stepped on a rock, and just as she stepped an arrow went through just after her face. Then they saw that the rock was attached to a system of machines that shot the arrow. Walking down the cave they heard a noise coming from a distance, they all rushed to the place and realised there were 6 wolves eating different body parts of a person. They were watching the wolves from a distance but by mistake, Andrew made a noise with his foot as he moved a rock. Listening to the voice the wolves stopped eating the human flesh and started looking from where the voice came from. Firstly, they were not seen by the wolves but Steve accidentally switched on the torch and the wolves started running towards the light. Jack and others decided to run to save their lives and they even successfully escaped. But later Steve realised that he had left his bag which contained all the food essentials at the place they were hiding to look after the wolves. They knew that they needed to get the bag back otherwise they would all start starving soon. As they went to the wolves' region again, they saw that the wolves were trying to tear the bag-pack but weren't able to. They decided that Andrew and Lana would go to the other side of the area to distract the wolves, Andrew threw a stone toward the wolves which distracted the wolves and they started running towards Andrew and Lana which provided time for Steve and Jack to get the bag-pack and rushed back again. Andrew and Lana returned safely as well.

They explored the cave and didn't find any ores and minerals so they all went to the place where they saw the rope going all the way down to the bottom. They didn't realise that this was the worst thing they could do in the journey going all the way down to the bottom. As they started to go down with the rope the rope started to shake. Lana went to the bottom first and later jack and Andrew came but as Steve was going to grab the rope, he saw a black figure standing just behind him and cause of this he started to panic which resulted in him slipping and he got fell to the bottom and he hit his head to a rock at the bottom which resulted in killing Steve. Jack and others started to cry after seeing Steve's dead body but for a second Andrew looked upwards with his flashlight and he saw a creepy figure at the top for a fraction of a second. It was the same figure which was standing behind Steve.

They decided to climb up the rope but as they grabbed the rope it broke; they realised that now they can't climb up again so they need to find a new exit. They left Steve's body at the spot and started to look for an exit. Just walking after two minutes they saw a plank above a gap between two ends, the plank was so light that it couldn't resist more than one person at a time, they crossed the plank one by one and continued their journey, just a minute later they saw something written on the wall of the cave in another language, Lana knew around 20 languages and she realised that the language was Hindi and she read the sign which said that 'जो आता है वही मरता है' she translated the message and told the other's that it means that:- 'the one who comes is the one who dies', they all started to tremble again, as they started walking again they saw a door with key hanging on its right side, Jack opened the door and they entered in a room which had names of the people carved on the wall who have come to this cave, later Jack noticed that Steve's name is also written on the wall but they were shocked because Steve was already dead so who wrote his name then they realised that the person with a creepy body has carved his name on the wall. They realised that they were in danger and needed to leave the room but the entry gate was now locked and they saw a narrow opening from which they decided to escape. As they escaped, they entered another room which had bodies of around 30 people and they also saw Steve's body as well. They left that room also and were tired now but they couldn't stop to take rest because they were still in danger.

They continued their search and saw a flash of light, they thought that it was the exit of the cave and got excited because of this they started running but due to excitement, Andrew fell into a gap having sharp spikes which resulted in killing Andrew as well. While they were facing the trauma of Steve's death, now they've faced one more. As they were looking towards Andrew's body, they saw that creepy figure again and ran but they were not fast enough as they were the tired cause of which they were caught by the creepy person. The person injected them which fainted Lana and Jack, As they came into their consciousness, jack asked why is the person killing everyone and the person replied that "a few years back, I also came to search the cave for ores and minerals with my colleagues but we encountered the wolves which killed my friends' cause of which I ran towards the opening back and screamed for help, but no one came to help then I decided that whoever comes to search this cave will end up dead", just after the person shot Lana and was about to shoot Jack, he woke up and realised that this was just a nightmare and was happy that his friends are still alive. Just then he received a letter from his friend Steve which he had written that they needed to explore a new cave on the order of their boss Peter in Florida. Jack started to tremble once again because we all know why.

Chapter 5

LIFE ON MARLY

Avisha Chaubey

Once upon a time there lived a girl named Claudia. She was a very curious, kind and helpful girl. She lived in a small family and had a few friends. She wasn't able to sleep at night, so she went to her balcony and sat there and she thought, "People should keep their surroundings clean. There is so much pollution, there is scarcity of water everywhere, but we don't take care of it. I wish I could do something about it. I would be very happy."

She looks up at the sky and suddenly she feels that a star is coming very close to her and it is staring at her and is listening to her. Then the star asked, "May I help you?" Then Claudia said, "Yes, but why?" "Because you are thinking about something great", said the star. "Okay, why not?" said Claudia. She was very happy and her eyes started gleaming. Then the star said, "Here, I'll give you some golden wings, but only on one condition. If you'll be affectionate and light-hearted to others, only then will the wings work."

Claudia readily agreed with the star's words. She

was thoroughly ecstatic. Then for hours and hours she stared at her wings with her shining eyes and wondered, "What shall I do with it?" Then suddenly an idea struck in her mind, "What if I could make my own world out of it, everything will be as I want." Then she made a planet and named it Marly. Then she told her family and friends about the planet, they couldn't believe it, they said, "How can this happen?" Then Claudia told them the whole story and took them to Marly. They were astonished.

Now they all live in Marly. Slowly, the days started passing by and everything was going very well, everyone living there was very happy, everyone's life was very good. But now there was a drastic change in Claudia's nature, she felt that she could do everything. There is no person like her in the world. Now her nature was not good, even with her family and friends and the person who made Marly, also kept it dirty. Now the power of her golden wings was gone.

When one day Claudia wanted to fly she was unable to fly. Then Claudia wondered, "Why aren't my golden wings working?" And suddenly the same star showed her again. And she remembered all the old things that the star had said to her, she realised that wherever we live, the environment around us should be kept clean and help others too. We don't need any magic wings to do anything.

"There is a magic power inside everyone, we just need to feel it..." She realised her mistake and she again started helping others like before and kept Marly clean as well. They all lived happily.

Chapter 6

Her Multiple Faces

Asmita Shrivastava

He tiredly opened his eyes and felt heavy as if bricks were kept upon his eyes. Blinking twice, he tried to adjust his sight with the beam of light hitting straight on his face. He found himself in an unfamiliar room, he panicked more when he saw a shadow stepping into the room. His body trembled with fear but it wasn't someone Shinichi was expecting it to be. It was just a simple girl wearing a cute, child-like pink dress, with a teddy bear in her hands held tightly in her arms. She looked at Shinichi with confusion all over her face but soon her eyes widened in shock as she just ran away without saying anything. "Hey! Please help me, young lady!!" He cried but got no answer from the back.

The boy slept with an empty stomach that day.

A rush of water got splashed all over his face, and he woke up panting and looked up at the person. A woman covered in all-black clothes glared at him, her face would shine with glory if that mask wasn't an interruption.

"W-Who? Who are you? And that little girl, where's she?"

"SHUT UP"

He got taken aback by her shouting. She grabbed a fistful of his hair and made him look into her eyes as she warns him-

"Stay away from her"

"Her…"

"What's so special about her?"

"Is she her mother? But I'm the victim, why would I harm her?" Shinichi thought to himself, being all puzzled. His stomach growled with hunger as he just sighed helplessly. But soon someone entered the room quietly with soft paws. She brought him food which was calling his name.

"You- Who are you? I saw you the other day too..."

"I-I am Tori"

She said sheepishly. Shinichi was mesmerised when he saw her properly.

"I'm so sorry for her behaviour she- she- she just doesn't like you… "What did I do? Did I ever hurt you? Even accidentally?" Shinichi asked softly as he sensed something was wrong with the girl.

"N-No S-She is just jealous-lous because I-I like you"

She confessed as a pink tint was visible all over her

face. Shinichi was in shock too but smiled with joy and looked at her, she giggled and left timidly. Shinichi grinned and slept on the floor.

Since then she would come to meet Shinichi every day and tell him her cute childish stories. He would listen to them with interest. With each day going by he fell in love with her more and more.

One day Tori didn't show up at Shinichi's room but instead someone else. In desperation, Shinichi thought it was Tori and started approaching the shadow unaware of the danger. It was the black girl. Anger and jealousy were visible in her eyes.

"I warned you, didn't I?" she whispered as she grinned evilly

"Look I love her, and I'll protect her no matter what. Now, you stay away from her. You got that?"

"LIAR"

She attacked him like a tigress. They fought like crazy, she punched him, and Shinichi dodged and punched her in defence. Her mask fell off giving Shinichi the biggest shock

It was Tori...since the very beginning

He was confused but still in love, he tried to approach her but she snatched away in disgust

"Who are you? Stay back...I said STAY BACK" Her head hurted like crazy and soon she fainted. It was all so messy for Shinichi but then it all made sense to him.

Tori had Multiple Personality Disorder.

He covered his mouth with his palm in shock, this was too much for him to digest. He took her in his arms to her room and laid her on her bed. As soon as he was about to leave a thing drop down catching his attention, it was a dairy. "Mari-San", it said, curious Shinichi started to read it and found out it was Tori's diary and her real name is Mari-San. At first, it seemed like a diary of a cheerful girl but slowly it turned dark, with sentences that reflected her sorrowful heart and disgust in her head for this cruel world.

"She's so brave. She fought...a lot, but guess she gave up now."

Shinichi commented as tears came running from his eyes. Mari slowly unfolded her eyes and found herself with an unfamiliar man in her room which made her jump a little in shock.

"Ahh Who are you? How did you end up in my room? You pervert!"

"Ahhhhh you scared me, O-Oh I-I am Shinichi."

Mari was perplexed, but Shinichi remained patient and provided a detailed explanation from start to finish. Although it was difficult for Mari to comprehend, Shinichi made it clear that she needed urgent assistance.

"Why should I trust you? What if you're like... others?"

"No Mari I'm not like others. I fell in love with your purest form, your little form, I can never in my life think like that."

As Mari looked into his tear-filled eyes, she knew that he was sincere and truly cared for her. With his encouragement, she sought professional help, attended counseling sessions, and took prescribed medication as needed. In time, things began to improve and return to normal. In the end, everything worked out well, as it often does in stories where tears are replaced by smiles and sadness is replaced by joy.

Chapter 7

THE MUMBLING TREE

(The Only Witness of Kala-Pani)

Saanvi

As we are celebrating "AZADI KA AMRIT MAHOSTAV", the glory of success, of 75 years of Independence, years of our beloved country with great pomp and show.

And, this year (2022), the theme of Independence Day is "NATION FIRST, ALWAYS FIRST". So, on this occasion, I decided to pen down my voyage to Andaman & Nicobar Islands.

My long cherished dream of visiting the Andaman & Nicobar Islands finally came true when we planned to celebrate our New Year in Port Blair. Filled with excitement and hope for good weather, we journeyed to Port Blair on the appointed day, eager as busy bees to begin our adventure.

The flight to Port Blair wasn't smooth as we faced turbulence during the flight. By God's grace, we landed safely at Veer Savarkar International Airport, Port Blair and reached our accommodation. A lovely property, with rooms that overlooked the brilliant blue waters of the Bay of Bengal.

Our first stop of the day was the Samudrika Naval Marine Museum where we saw a variety of fish and twinkling corals. A quiet and beautifully maintained place. It gave us an insight into not just marine life but also the history, and geographical information about the various tribes. Afterwards, we visited Corbyn's Cove Beach, Anthropological Museum and so on.

We also visited Chatham Saw Mill. Asia's largest and oldest saw mill. And I bought artefacts as a souvenir from the mill.

On the second day, we visited the Historic Ross Island and North Bay Island. We enjoyed exploring Ross Island by walking ways through it. We were lucky to see the spotted deer, rabbits, peacocks and crabs there. And the funniest part was to run with the herds of spotted deer.

North Bay Island is one among the best locations for Scuba Diving, Sea Walk, Snorkeling and many more water activities. Infringed with rich coral reefs, this island is visited by a lot of travellers each day. A certified diver was present with every single person to take care of the person and to navigate through the beautiful world of the UnderWater Life.

Here, I tried my hand in snorkelling, watching marine life at such close quarters was an out of the world experience as we came back feeling overwhelmed. We were wondering if it was so beautiful near the shore, how much more amazing it would be a little deeper into the sea.

I was filled with immense joy as I witnessed my Nemo world come to life, with a beautiful shoal of Zebra fish and an Octopus snuggled up in its cozy abode. It was an incredible experience that words cannot fully capture.

Next up, was the crown jewel of Andaman - Radha Nagar Beach at Havelock Island, a paragon of beauty, these islands present a landscape of scenic and picturesque extravaganza, shimmering like emeralds in the Bay of Bengal where the beach wasn't just limited to the white sand and the blue waters.

Radhanagar beach was so clean and the sand was so comfortable that we ended up just walking barefoot on the beach with the waves swishing and swirling around us. The most lovable part of each and every child's dream is making sand castles and for sure, I'm not the exception. I made many sand castles and enjoyed playing with sand.

The next morning, we were supposed to visit Elephant Beach, but unfortunately, there was a call of an unexpected Cyclone. And all the tourists had to immediately vacate the place. We all were worried after hearing the disasters of Cyclone from the locals.

The Rescue Operation had been launched and we all were standing in long queues to board the Indian Naval Ships and the local cruises guarded by Coast Guard Officers. And everyone was in a panic to board the ships and cruise to save themselves which is a hard challenge to the officers to handle the people. Now each and every citizen's safety was their responsibility. The ride back to Port Blair with torrential downpour was a bit bumpy this time, as we were sailing against the waves. By God's grace and salute to the sailors, after so many hurdles we docked in Port Blair.

This was a journey we all will never forget for the rest of our lives. The memories are still fresh in our mind, especially the experience of snorkelling, jet ski and visiting one of the most beautiful beaches ever i.e. Radha Nagar Beach was awesome. Here I will put an end to the story but the journey still continues.

It was evening and near the dock there was the Cellular Jail, a National Memorial. I heard people mumbling about a tree narrating a story about Kala-pani. I was so curious to know about the Mumbling Tree, Kala-Pani !!!????????????

While standing in the queue for the tickets Mommy told me, "It's a pilgrimage destination for freedom fighters, also known as Kala-Pani". This colossal edifice has mutely witnessed the most treacherous of inhumane atrocities borne by the convicts, who were mostly freedom fighters.

And to capture the minute history and details of that era, I walked into the complex expecting to see a dark and dingy place echoing the anguished cries of all the people who were housed there for years. But what we walked into was a bright and shining courtyard with an occasional dark cloud crossing over ready with a light and sound show explained through A Mumbling Tree standing tall, ever since. Many notable independence activists including Vinayak Damodar Savarkar were imprisoned here during the struggle for freedom from The British Rule.

The story being narrated by the voice of an ancient Peepal tree is refreshing. The entire show brings up the dark history of the islands and reminds us exactly why these beautiful islands were once called Kala-Pani.

The saga of the islands' adversities was brought alive inside the jail compound and it lasted around 45 minutes. The show was a spectacle of colourful lights with a very engaging commentary. It is a perfect blend of both information and entertainment. For sure, it is to kindle the inner patriot in us. But it left us speechless and drowned us into tears for the hardships faced by the prisoners and their struggles.

Today is a day to feel proud about being a part of

this great nation. May this spirit of freedom lead us all to success and glory in life. Let's keep the memories and A big salute to all the people who sacrificed their lives for our nation!

So let's celebrate "Azadi Ka Mahotsav", with great zeal and zest to bring alive stories of unsung heroes whose sacrifices have made freedom a reality for us and also revisit the milestones, freedom movements etc. In the Historical Journey to 15 August, 1947.

Jai Hind !

Azadi Ka Amrit Mahotsav

Chapter 8

ALEX - THE BRUTAL KING

Harsimrat Kaur

Once there lived Alex, a ruthless king of a big empire. His great, brutal army had helped him in conquering any land coming his way, resulting in extending his empire to far places. People used to call him, "the invincible King" as no one had ever defeated him. Whenever his huge army moved, either the rival kings ran away to save their lives or surrendered their monarch to save their people from the merciless army of Alex. Those days every king used to pray to God to save their kingdom from coming to the notice of Alex.

One day, Alex was getting ready to go on a quest of invading a smaller kingdom hidden behind a mountain range. Then, something unexpected happened which was going to change the fate of the invincible Alex Alex' beloved son Thomas suddenly got severely ill. He wasn't opening his eyes and was struggling for every breath. Alex had never cared for anyone except his son. Brutal Alex was unexpectedly a good father and loved his son a lot. But, now the only person whom he loved was dying in front of his eyes. Thomas was suffering from an incurable disease. Alex couldn't watch his son struggling for his every breath. Alex' wife and queen Etrina blamed him and said that it was the result of all his sins which had now come as a curse for their child. She believed that God was punishing him for all the bad deeds he did in his whole life. After watching his child's suffering, Alex became insane and more brutal. He killed every physician in his kingdom as they had failed to cure his dying son. Soon, he ordered his guards to abduct all the best physicians from other kingdoms and present them before him.

Later, after four days the guards presented before him the twelve best physicians. The abducted men were the most proclaimed physicians from other kingdoms, famous for saving many lives. Alex said if his son dies, then he will kill every physician and asked if they want to leave the place alive then they had to save his son's life. Every physician was given a bag containing all kinds of herbs to prepare any medicine. Soon those miserable and scared magicians of medicine started preparing something to save Alex' son's life as well as their own. At night, they all presented before him some medicines except one physician named Antonio. Antonio didn't come with any medicine.

King Alex got extremely angry to see Antonio with

empty hands and said, "Soo you are not interested in saving your life, but don't think I will give you an easy death!"

"King Alex I have seen this incurable illness earlier," Antonio replied. "I want to tell you a harsh truth, no medicine prepared by my fellow physicians or anyone is enough to save your son's life so I felt worthless to prepare anything."

"Oh! you know everything about my child's illness, so tell me where you had seen this disease earlier and what happened to your patient, did he die like my son is dying right now?" Alex asked in his angry voice.

"No he survived, and right now that patient is standing in front of you," Antonio replied.

"What do you mean? " Alex asked.

"I was that patient who had suffered this disease when I was a young boy and my father had saved my life," Antonio replied.

"Don't try to puzzle me, explain to me everything clearly how your father had saved you otherwise I am barely holding myself to take your life at any moment.

Antonio replied, "King Alex I know you will not kill me at least until something happens to your son as I know, right now my life is more valuable after your son."

"Yes", Alex said, "you are right, this is the reason

you are still alive and talking to me but not so long. If one more time you tried to puzzle me, I will take your life right now".

"I'm not here to puzzle you," Antonio said, "so you want to know how my father saved my life, then listen. He sacrificed his life to save me."

What sacrifice?" Alex asked, but this time in a dull voice, "What are you talking about? Tell me clearly?"Antonio said, "Outside this kingdom in the jungles of Onuma, grows rare black mushrooms that can save your child's life from this incurable disease."

After hearing that, the king promptly ordered his guards to bring every black-looking mushroom present in the jungle.

Antonio said, "King Alex wait, I have to tell you something else!"

"I am listening to you," Alex replied, "what do you want more, just tell me?"

Antonio explained the dilemma to the king, "Your son can only be saved by you or the queen eating the rare mushroom. After eating it, you need to give some drops of your blood to the ill person's mouth for five days. However, the catch is that on the sixth day, the person who ate the mushroom will die due to the poison present in it. But, the patient will be completely cured."

"Oh! So this sacrifice you were talking about," the King replied to Antonio and asked his guards to call the queen. Antonio again elaborated everything to the queen. Queen Etrina said, "Dear king Alex have you forgotten, I'm not your child's actual mother, you had killed his mother many years ago for deceiving you." For the first time, the king felt he was not invincible and God was really punishing him for his bad deeds. He soon ordered his guards to release everyone and went to Thomas's room. The abducted physician hurriedly left the place except Antonio, who followed Alex to his son's room. Antonio saw him crying, regretting, confessing all his sins and blaming himself for his child's sufferings. At night the guards came with those rare black mushrooms. Alex ate those mushrooms and dropped some of his blood into his son's mouth by cutting his hand. Thomas soon started getting better every day and opened his eyes on the fifth day, but on the sixth-day king Alex died leaving all his great empire for the future king.

Finally, the brutal king got defeated by his own fate, but a great father won.

Chapter 9

THE RIGHT WAY TO LIVE

Aditi Singh

I can't believe I will soon be with my family and be able to have dinner with them. After spending four days on an island where each day felt like a whole year, the only thing that I wish is to be with my loved ones.

You might be wondering how an eighteen-year-old girl ended up being on a deserted island. Well, just a few days ago, I was just a seventeen-year-old girl, excited about turning eighteen very soon. It was 11th November, the day before my birthday. I had a flight the next day to France, a place that I have always wanted to visit since I was four. As I was almost eighteen, I decided that I'll go on a solo trip. Though excited, I was also scared and nervous as I had never been to another country alone. I couldn't sleep that night thinking about how I would be in my dream country a few hours later.

Next day, I waved a good bye to my family at the airport unaware of the challenges right ahead of me. It was 5am when I boarded the plane which means I would reach Paris by 2pm to 3pm.

It was a smooth flight. I had my brunch at 12. But suddenly the weather started deteriorating and dark clouds covered the whole sky. I assumed it was just a small turbulence. The air hostess asked the passengers not to panic and stay calm. After an hour or so, the plane started shaking vigorously. Everyone was scared and puzzled. I too became restless and negative thoughts took over my mind. We were asked to stay in our seats and buckle up our seat belts. Later, there was an announcement by the captain that the plane's engine was damaged due to the storm and that we might have to do an emergency landing into the ocean. The air hostess gave us certain instructions about oxygen masks and life jackets. At that point, all I could think about was my friends, family and all my dreams. With my teary eyes, I looked at other passengers, all terrified. I closed my eyes and remembered all the precious moments that I had spent with my parents knowing very well that I might never be able to see them or hug them ever again.

All of a sudden, we could feel the plane going down at a very high speed. It was shaking. Everyone was screaming and praying. I thought of my parents and all the memories I had created with them. After that the only thing I remember is that there was a loud noise and it was all dark around. I felt dizzy and soon became unconscious.

After a few hours, I woke up to the sound of waves. My head hurt like I had been shot in my head. With a blurry vision, I looked all around me. It took me a few minutes to recollect all that had happened. I looked at the other people who lay lifeless in their seats. It was a horrifying sight. I unbuckled my seatbelt and tried to get up. I couldn't walk properly. My leg was badly hurt. Somehow, I managed to get out of my seat. There was sand all over. I guessed that we might have landed on an island. With a hope to get out of the plane, I headed towards the door. But there was no door. The front portion of the plane was broken and buried in sand. I didn't know what to do. I headed to the emergency exit and after struggling for an hour or so, I finally came out. It was already dark. But the fire caused by that plane crash lit up the environment. The ocean was right in front of me. For some reason, the sound of waves scared me. It was just me, the ocean and that silence. As I looked at the ocean, I heard my stomach rumbling. I was hungry. So, I went into the plane again to search for some food. I looked in each and every passenger's bag. And thankfully I could find enough food to survive a day or two. I found a half-eaten chocolate bar. I had never been so delighted to see chocolate ever before in my life. It tasted extra good that day.

I decided to stay inside the plane and wait till the sunrise. I went back to my seat. As I sat there, I thought of all the moments that I didn't get to spend with my loved ones, regretting every time I fought with my parents. I wished that I had stayed home and celebrated my eighteenth birthday with them. But I also knew that I had to get out of that island alive.

Next day, I woke up and rushed to find some kind of cloth to make a tent. I couldn't stay in the plane forever. I used all my knowledge of survival that I had taken from the television shows and movies. I found some blankets that the passengers might have used. I combined them to make a large piece of cloth. Then, I went to find some wooden logs to make a tent.

After hours of work and failing quite a few times, I succeeded in making a shelter for myself. It was not the best but I was proud of it. I realised that it would get dark very soon and I'll need fire to keep myself warm. The fire would also attract the attention of ships passing by. So I went to look for some dry wood. I remembered the episode of man vs wild where he taught to light fire using two pieces of wood. By the time I lit the fire, it was already night. I suddenly realised that I hadn't celebrated my birthday. Because of the plane crash I completely forgot about it. I really missed my house. But I was happy that at least I was alive. I imagined the leftover sandwich that a person might have ordered during the flight, to be my birthday cake and sang a birthday song to myself. I was so tired that I didn't even realise when I had fallen asleep.

The next few days passed the same way. In all these days, I had multiple breakdowns and the thought of giving up crossed my mind almost every day. But then I remembered my parents, how happy they would be to see me alive and that kept me alive. It was today, that is, 15th of November, that there was finally a ray of hope. I saw a small ship heading towards the island. They must have seen the remains of the plane. I was so happy. Tears flowing down my cheeks, I smiled. Never had I ever been so happy in my entire eighteen years of life. The fact that I would soon be with my family made me cry even harder. I shouted and waved at the ship.

Now that I head to my house, sitting in this old ship with a bunch of strangers, writing this story, I realise how much I have learnt in all these days that I spent on that island. This experience, though terrible, made me realise how much those little things in life that we take for granted actually mean to us. Having dinner with family, going out with friends, being able to spend precious moments of life with them, all these things seem so small but when they are gone and we are away from them, we realise the real joy behind them. Our phone, laptops and technology that we think we cannot live without are actually not that important. The joy that I got when I had that leftover chocolate, made me understand the importance of everything that I have in my life. If we ever think about it then we'll realise that we already have enough to live on this planet and that instead of running after more and more, we should cherish what we have right now because who knows if we'll be able to live those moments again.

Chapter 10

THE WORLD OF MAGIC POWERS

Aradhya Agarwal

The world holds power that you don't know about.

I went for a morning walk then I saw a camera-like lens in the blue sky pointed towards me. As soon as the thought of hiding struck me, my body started to vanish, and blacked out in a matter of a few seconds. My eyes opened to see a completely new world and saw a bearded man in white clothing.

I got goosebumps hearing the low-pitched voice of the man say, "Welcome to the world of Great Powers!"

My mouth opened wide. "W-where am I? In the world of great powers?

W-what!!"

The master said, "You are one of the Protectors to protect me and you have the power of Invisibility which will work when you think to be invisible with great focus."

I had mixed feelings at that moment. I was shocked and very happy too that I had been chosen to protect him but I didn't know him, so I asked him, "But who are you and who are the other protectors?"

The master responded, "I am the master of great powers, The other protectors are James and Jennifer."

After this conversation, I was teleported back to earth.

I contacted the other two protectors and we made sure no one knew about our powers.

After a few days, we were normally walking on the road until we saw a camera-like lens.

I remembered that this is the same camera that I saw when I was walking and the master also told me that this is the camera that is released by Akshay to find out our Identity and power. The camera was constantly following us. That's when we realised, they already knew our identity and powers as all three of us were together.

Then after a few hours, we tried to contact the master but we weren't able to or either go to their world.

The next day I met my Best Friend Charles. he was so surprised when he saw me, he jumped and I don't know how but he suddenly went to the rooftop and then his body and face started to change and he was maintaining distance with me he told me that I am his enemy I was shocked then I remembered that master told me that his Enemy Akshay Kumar also has 3 protectors so I realised that one of them is Charles and he has the power of speed I was very scared and sad that I will be fighting with my best friend but suddenly he attacked me his other 2 mates who were the other two protectors came and we started fighting. I also started fighting with them. I gave a signal to my other mates (the other 2 protectors who were with me) . We had a long fight. At one moment we all disappeared and I and my other two mates were with the master and my friend Charles and his other two mates were with Akshay Kumar. Our Master taught us some tricks so we can defeat them. After an hour suddenly our land of the world started to vibrate. Everything was falling and our enemies appeared and had a really bad fight. I had the power to be invisible, Jennifer had the power of fire and James had the power to read people's minds. Our enemies had the power of water, speed, and strength. We used all the techniques that the master told us and we were about to defeat them but we couldn't kill Charles as he had the power of speed every time we used to go near him he used to run but at last, guess what I became invisible and told Jennifer to be behind me we caught Charles and he was also dead We all were very Happy but suddenly Akshay Kumar came and told in a hoarse voice, "You were correct in your way and we were correct in our ways you shouldn't have killed my protectors they very kind-hearted"

Then our master came and said, "That's true that we were correct and you too but you started the and we should complete it. Your protectors were monsters. We are glad that they are being killed if they would be in this world and people would not be able to survive. If you become a good person like us then you can join our world where we are not monsters, we are kind-hearted and help people"

Akshay Kumar responded," Sure I would love to be in your world. It would be a little difficult for me to leave the world of Monsters but it would be kind of us to help other people."

Chapter 11

AN AVERAGE STUDENT

Sania Firoz

I just came home from school and had my PT3 exam and the date sheet of my pre boards has already come. I am so fed-up of giving exams one after another. The school thinks this is helping us by preparing for our boards but this is just creating tension and anxiety for the students. In order to score well I usually focus on mugging up the concepts instead of understanding them. This makes me get all confused between different concepts. This leads to me not scoring well and eventually getting depressed and to me comparing myself to the people who have scored higher than me.

1 WEEK BEFORE THE EXAM

For the past few weeks I have not even slept. This is what my life has come to. I just want to go back to my childhood days and want to play carelessly and just want to get my 8 full hours of sleep. OK, enough daydreaming I need to do Math's. But at the same time I don't want to do Math. Now it's basically turned into a staring competition between the Maths textbook and me and no one is about to give up. But because of this harsh world in which the god and the creator of exams is against every student, I need to study and score well so I can show everyone my true potential.

ON THE DAY OF EXAM

I am feeling very nervous and anxious. I have been preparing for this preboard for over a month and still am feeling that I will not score well . My mind says that I am fully prepared but my heart says the opposite and I don't know who to follow . Some people say to follow your heart but the remaining say to follow your mind . This is a disadvantage for us normal , average human beings . we can't make a single decision. Imagine if everyone could make one same , single decision. Life would have been so easy. To top it all of my parents are not even helping me with this exam . I swear to god if I ever become a parent, I will ensure that my children will not go through the same situation as me . OK enough overthinking let me just revise for the exam.

GIVING THE EXAM

Sin2B + Cos2B = 1…… What in the world is this ? This is the problem with me . I completely blank out when I am giving an exam. 5 marks down the drain. I loved maths in my childhood but in sixth class I faced a downfall. There was a chapter known as Algebra , I despise it . like why in the world maths needs to add alphabets . I thought alphabets were meant for English. OK moving on , next question . "A boy buys 1000 umbrellas" ………… Just being curious but why does a boy need 1000 umbrellas! Is he preparing for a tsunami? Maths really said "logic went out the window".

AFTER GIVING THE EXAM

Silence please, I need some peace after giving that terrible exam . Everyone is so happy even the person who has scored the lowest in all of the 10th. I don't know how someone can be this happy after giving a maths exam. It's like seeing people who have topped in CBSE Board Exam 2022-2023 but I am really worried about myself .

ON THE DAY OF RESULT

Oh again I have scoreless marks , I have to face the scowl faces of my parents. and my teachers will be telling me the same thing that I didn't work to my potential. I wish I could throw this piece of crap but I can't. Being an average student no one can really recognize you easily if you want to be recognized. The student needs to work hard so that you would be the speaker of the program. I think I am a good speaker but some people haven't recognized my potential.

Today I score one of the least marks in maths and got the fattest tears of my life the worst part of scoring less marks is not the scolding that you get it is the eye contact that you get from others the inner laughing face but from outside the sympathy that is shown it looks like that they are my true friends. I really hate the concept of group studying because it is only good when you have true friends and I feel it is the main reason for my sad life. I really miss my childhood. There was no comparison, competition and I wish I could really live that moments my entire life being in a high school everyone is having expectations except some of those extraordinary position holders. I think they have decided what we will be doing in our future.

But it's time to prove them wrong the person who know your potential is the person within yourself I know I will prove all those position holders wrong I feel the biggest competitors of me today is the past that I have lived I know where to improve and the time when you understand this always remember you are halfway done to succeed.

After 4 months

Today was the day when the crowd was waiting

to laugh but its time for them to eat sweets. It is 12 of march 2022 at 3 :oo pm results were out and I was sleeping and woke up with 12 missed calls the crowd members must be thinking that I haven't pass but I can broadly say I have got 90 percent and 95 in maths I feel like if a person who scored 45 can score 95 also you just need to listen your thoughts that are coming from inner you. I won't much give credits to others but I feel I have came a long way I won't say it was the highest score but it was my potential that I gave . After this I got to learn one very important point of life "love yourself first " everyone is going to judge you for your work whether it is good or bad but you need to trust and love yourself first . I will never ever forget the marks that I scored in pre boards as it has taught me a lot of things. I feel like we should always "Appreciate the good moments with some bad ones" as bad moments tell us more than the good ones, it just boosts your ego.

Chapter 12

Her Tears and Their Souls

Aanya Sangar

There was dust. Smoke. Fire. The air was filled with such an amount of smoke that she coughed so hard, her lungs felt as though they tore apart every time she did. She screamed out loud because her arms were hurting so much; it felt like they were dying. Her eyes were barely open, and she could feel this weight on her that was killing her. On her waist, on her legs, on her chest. She started dragging herself from beneath it, although there was no strength in her. It was difficult; difficult to wake up in a cave with a giant rock resting on her and coughing like a maniac, trying to free herself.

It was difficult to remember that she might not even find her parents after escaping this giant rock, let alone find herself some food. After a struggle of 15 minutes, she pushed herself out and fell on the hard, cemented surface. She stumbled up and opened her eyes fully. There was cold, terrified sweat on her face and her hair was in a bun although it wasn't helping her look around because it was all over her eyes. She was covered in blood and sweat. Sweat was dripping from her body and clothes. There was soot and dirt all over her, covering her face and her clothes. Rubbing her eyes, she walked towards the other end of this cave, waiting to see her beloved town, wrecked to pieces.

The place was filled with bulldozer-sized rocks and there was fire burning here and there. It was really hot and congested here because of the fire. The smoke was filling her lungs so that every time she breathed, she would cough out as though she had stage-4 lung cancer. It was better not to breathe. She wondered why there wasn't a way that she could not breathe and still be alive. The place was scary. Eerie and wicked. It was too dark, and the only source of light was the fire. The smoke and dust and rocks and fire, all things which existed on Earth, did not make it better for her. She was rather more scared because of them and wished she was on an alien planet rather than to be here.

She walked around, breathing heavily and panting, just in case some evil came at her to kill her. She was walking around gingerly when her feet stepped on a slimy yet hard thing. Nonplussed, she looked down and to her astonishment, screamed so loud, her voice echoed around. She had stepped on a human corpse, melted because of the fire. Gasping and panting all the while, she stared at it although she didn't want to. She hated this thing which was lying there but she couldn't keep her eyes off. It was when a rock fell beside her that she was brought back to reality and started moving, stepping on all those melted corpses, flinching all the while.

Linda was a 13-year-old girl. She had long blonde hair and light brown eyes. She had bold eyes filled with beauty and grace and her nose was thin and sharp. She had a sharp jawline, making her much more attractive. She had always been a happy-go-lucky and calm girl. She was really loving and caring for those who were close and important to her.

But something terrifying had happened to her and not only her, but to the town of Indianapolis, to the whole state of Indiana, to the whole USA. There was destruction of life, of property, of nature. There was a war.

The USA and Russia have been known to be deadly rivals for more than 30 years. Of course, it was possible for Russia to send an army of 50,000 commies, bomb the different states of the country and kill a million of people randomly after 30 years.

Linda walked for another hour or so that she saw a streak of light from the rocks caving the place. Mustering with all her courage she started pushing them away with a long wooden stick. She was exhausted to the core and had no idea how she was doing this, but she was doing it with the thought of meeting her sister and her parents. The light was pouring in on her, blinding her slowly by every second. The largest rock fell, and light hit her eyes after what felt like ages. She covered her eyes for about 10 minutes, walking around, astounded at what had happened.

There were still more bodies, thousands of them lying there, all of them killed by the bomb blast. By some miracle, she had survived, and it wasn't an easy save. Her arms were burnt and there were deep cuts here and there. She stumbled around here and there panting, wishing not to see a loved one lying there, dead. She was walking around when she saw a blinding white light.

"You survived! Are you-are you okay?!"

The person pulled away and Linda, with difficulty, stopped covering her eyes.

He had that specific teenage vibe about him. His face was glowing with hot sweat and his eyes were wide and inquiring. His hair was completely messed up and there was a deep burn on his neck. His face, his hands, everything, was covered in cuts and scars and blood.

"I did. Have you seen mom and dad?" she asked, scared.

"No. No, God, no I haven't! It's scaring me, I haven't even seen my own parents!"

His hands were in his hair, then reaching down and holding his neck, a terrified look all along. He was Linda's most trusted friend.

"The ambulances have arrived."

He pointed at some distance beside her that she saw injured people being taken to the hospital. A lot were dead. They started walking, feeling the fearing vibes passing through them.

"How many died? What do you think?" she asked.

"Thousands. Millions. Billions all over America!"

"And we survived. Out of all those billions." Linda said, suddenly grateful. He just gave her a small smile.

They walked a little more distance until they saw two bodies. Two bodies covered in blood and… not alive. Not breathing. Dead.

"Oh no… Linda, I'm so sorry!" Cried Matthew, hugging her, pulling away his eyes from the two dead bodies.

She couldn't feel anything. Not even Matthew hugging her. Not the cold wind hitting her face. What is this? What is happening? They aren't dead, surely they aren't. They're just unconscious; her parents can't die. They can't leave her like this alone in the world.

Why was Matthew acting like this? But it wasn't before 2 rescuers looked at her with tear-filled eyes that she realised. That it knocked her off, that she felt like falling deep in this dark hole, pulling her in, pulling her with such strength that she could not do anything but go deeper and deeper, her heart filling with huge weight. She could just stand there and gasp, her eyes already filling with the tears that her parents might not see again…

It had been three years. Indianapolis was slowly coming back to its normal state, it almost had. The economy had fallen to three-fourths and there had been huge property loss. But slowly everything was getting back to normal.

Linda and Matthew are 15 years old now. Linda had foster parents, but she was leading a quiet life. It was satisfying at least. Matthew and she had become closer, much closer for all their friends had died in the bomb blast. They had a new school now and she was enjoying her life a lot. She was good at studies, sports, and music. Everything was just the way it should have been.

But wherever she went, whatever she did… she could feel a heavy weight on her… a weight that sometimes pulled her down, stopping her from doing what was necessary… and whenever this happened, she always wondered.

How is it that spreading peace is so hard but procuring guns is so easy?

Chapter 13

Once Upon an Epiphany

Lawanya Pandey and Avani Kulshreshtha

Idris had always been the kind of girl who looked at everything with negativity. For her the glass was always half empty. She always went on about how her job was too tiring, her salary too low, her house too small. Never did she ever try to appreciate the good things that happened around her.

Once, she was sitting in the park after a particularly rough day. She had been told off by her employer about how she always sulked around, and when she had tried to rant about this to her friend, he had said that her constant bickering was annoying.

And so she wondered about how happy she would have been if she had better friends and a better employer. She looked up at the sky and saw a large flock of birds flying above. Oh how she wished she were a bird. She would fly around without a care in the world. She was absolutely certain she would have been satisfied if she were a bird, living freely without any restrictions. Idris closed her eyes, wishing to be as unbound as a bird.

The next day when she woke up, Idris realised she

couldn't feel her hands. Or her feet. Or her face. She looked around and saw feathers where her hands were supposed to be! She couldn't believe her eyes. Her wish had come true. Idris really had turned into a bird! Her clenched jaw slowly turned into a smirk. Idris would finally live the life of her dreams, she would finally be satisfied with her life. There wouldn't be anyone or anything to disappoint her. She would go anywhere she wanted, anytime she wanted, and she wouldn't have to deal with her mundane routine.

And so she flew out the window and into the wide open blue. Idris soared over skyscrapers and the lakes. She peered down at the tiny humans. How happy she was to escape her imperfect life.

But before she went out and finally loved the life where she was satisfied, Idris had to do something about her growling stomach. She perched down on a tree and looked around to see if she could find something to eat. A few metres away she saw a restaurant. She could see some cooked rice lying in through the window. Perfect. She flew down to the window and entered the restaurant. Just as she was about to peck at the rice, a man came in and shooed her away. Idris flew out for her life and didn't look back. Defeated, she flew a little while in search of food, but there wasn't any where she could end her hunger without being chased down by a bunch of huge angry humans.

"Okay so maybe birds don't *really* have a perfect life," Idris thought to herself.

Just as she was about to take flight again in search of food, she saw an enormous eagle flying in towards her. It was a large mass of brown with vicious opal eyes. It was honed with an amber beak which was sharp enough to pierce through its prey. It was coming straight at Idris. She flew away in the opposite direction and flapped her wings briskly and dashed away in no time.

She flew through the river, across the skies and over the city but there was no place to go to. There was no place she could call home. No one she could talk to. She was starving, tired, restless, and the near-death experience had shook her completely. That feeling of freedom soon turned to fear and the boundless sky felt like a whole world which she had to navigate herself.

She soon realised how ignorant she had been to think that birds led a life with no difficulties. She had always thought that someone somewhere led a satisfactory and perfect life. Idris was hit with the fact that this was not true. Everyone had their own difficulties, their own responsibilities and imperfections. No one was perfect, and as hard as they tried, no one could ever be perfect. Idris realised that perfection didn't exist. She went on about how she didn't have what she deserved but never did she try to work towards achieving what she wanted. She was also so engrossed in herself that she didn't even notice the small gestures of kindness that humanity offered in this otherwise dark and unkind world. Did she ever thank her mother for doing her chores for her when she was in school? Did she ever thank her friends for being there for her in her darkest moments? Did she ever stop and appreciate the sheer beauty of the world? Idris realised she hadn't. It was the small thoughtful acts of kindness that made everyone go through their day, but Idris always focused on how she was always unsatisfied.

And so Idris wished to turn to a human again. She decided to go headfirst and see everything in a new light. She resolved to not complain about every little thing, and appreciate the people around her more. She would thank her mother, her friends, her employer, her milkman, every person who contributed to making sure that everyone lived a comfortable life. She couldn't unsay all the negative things she had said to others all these years, but she could at least thank them for being there for her, even if she hadn't appreciated their presence at the time.

The sound of the alarm clock in the morning woke Idris up. She didn't know if all of that was a dream, or if it had really happened. What she did know however, was that she was not the old Idris anymore. She had changed. For the better. She breathed in, put a smile on her face and decided that the first thing she'll do is thank her mother. And so she went.

And just as the door of her room closed behind her, a few brown feathers that were lying on the bed flew out through the window into oblivion.

Chapter 14

Nightmare on The Eldervalley Street

Dishi Jain

Could one call Eldervalley a normal small town? From the outside, no one would see anything interesting, different, wild but the people of Eldervalley knew the truth. This was a town cursed to miseries and sorrows. Why do people still stay there then? Well, the people who could afford to leave, left decades ago, only bloody businessmen and low lives stay here. This is a story from Eldervalley. A story that still lives in the hearts of the people. No one knows the truth, but everyone believes in a good lie.

Ella and Carter Grayson, twins at birth, and an inseparable duo. They were the children of Boham and Bellatrix Grayson. The wealthiest family in Eldervalley. Though blessed with wealth, the family wasn't known for its good reputation. Ella and Carter were the only ones who were slightly respected in the community.

They had a summerly ritual. To go camping in the neighbouring forest. Locals called it the weeping forest, many had died there due unexplainable reasons. But Ella and Carter had been doing this since they were kids. No creepy story was going to stall them. However this time, they were to be accompanied with their friends, Veronica, Paris, Oliver and Noah.

They were juniors, going into their senior years. To celebrate it, they decided to make this camping trip a little more interesting. Noah packed along a ouija board.

None of them believed in supernatural crap. They were quite the fearless group.

It was the 4th of July. Celebrations were being held all over time. Though a small backwards town, the people certainly knew how to party.

Noah, Paris, Oliver and Veronica met the twins at the Grayson residence. Huge and gothy, it had a certain charm to it.

"Got the drinks and food, Noah you got the board?" asked Oliver as he put down a sack of snacks on the floorboard.

"Indeed I do, my parents aren't too happy we're doing this. We should be careful!" replied Noah.

'I cannot believe my ears, Noah, the most fearless one out of us is saying this! Hallelujah!" exclaimed Paris, with the most surprised look on her rather small face.

The others chuckled while Noah sighed. He had a bad feeling in his guts about this.

"Alright then, we should get going." said Ella, looking at Carter to ask for his approval.

"Yeah, let's go!" said Carter with excitement in his tone.

In just half an hour, the group reached the forest, and their excitement was palpable. Noah's concerns melted away in the company of his joyful friends. Upon reaching the campsite, they were surprised to find an authorized area in this supposedly haunted forest. The group quickly unpacked and set up camp, but Noah struggled to light the bonfire. Despite his usual proficiency, there seemed to be no wind or other element to aid him.

Veronica, shivering in the chilly air, reminded Noah of the urgent need for warmth. "We'll freeze if you don't get this fire going," she chided. Frustrated, Noah lamented the weather, while the group sighed in disappointment. However, Ella and Carter insisted on turning the night around.

"Come on, guys, don't let this setback dampen our spirits," Ella urged. "We have plenty of warm clothes. Let's sing some karaoke and get this party started!"

KARAOKE GONE WRONG

In the midst of the weeping forest, one could hear the mainstream pop songs booming through the trees.

"God Oliver! What is stuck in your throat? You've defamed Shawn Mendes. My ears are actually going to bleed." said Paris, mockingly.

The group chuckled.

Laughs and songs, jokes and chuckles. They were having the time of their life.

Out of the blue, Paris and Veronica heard the bushes behind them rustling. A swift wind flew across their cold faces. A sudden haunted silence surrounded them.

"Did you guys hear that? What's happening?"

"What do you mean, Paris? Veronica? You two okay?" said Carter.

Veronica was seemingly frozen. Not a word spoken, neither a muscle moved.

"Earth to Veronica! What is up with you?"said Ella, as she shook Veronica by the arm.

"We need to get out of here. Right the hell now." said Veronica, as she shook herself back to life. She seemed to have seen something ghastly.

"Oh please Ver, what is up? Don't ruin the night." sighed Ella.

"Don't you guys see it?! We will all die. I'm getting out of here."

Veronica runs towards the car, when a high-pitched scream causes her to turn back.

“Oh my god Ella! What happened? What is going on?” screamed Paris.

Ella had been caught in a trap, she fell and her head hit a rock. Intensive bleeding followed.

The group panicked.

“I’m trying to tell you guys, I saw something, someone, behind the bushes. Dressed up in branches and twigs. This is dangerous territory. We need to get out. Oliver, Carter, get Ella up. We need to leave.” said Veronica.

RUN OR DIE

Without warning, two men emerged from the bushes. Dressed in animal fur and feathers and wielding a massive axe, they sent shivers down the group’s spines. Fear was evident on everyone’s faces.

The scarier of the two men spoke in a language that none of the group could recognize, let alone understand. A tense exchange ensued, but neither side could comprehend the other’s words.

“This is the worst situation to be in, we need to leave.” whispered Carter to Ella.

The men seemed to have noticed the not-so-subtle whispering. Their voices raised, violence seemed to be coming.

Bam! Out of nowhere, a brink smashed down onto

one of the men. It was Paris who threw the brick.

The other man ran before the group could do anything.

He was dead. The brick had caused such intensive damage, that he died on the spot.

"What have you done! He's dead, paris. Dead." screamed Veronica as she visibly panicked.

"What do you want me to do? They would have killed us! Did you guys not see them? The way they spoke? Did they look like good people?" said Paris.

"But that doesn't-" said Veronica as she was interrupted in between by Oliver.

"Paris is right, we don't need your moral policing right now. Leave the body here, who would even know? Let alone, who would care? Let's just leave." said Oliver.

The group nodded in agreement, They got in the car.

"What the hell, it won't start! There's fuel, the tires are fine. The engine is alright. Why won't it start?, said Noah in frustration.

"Well this is great. This night couldn't get any worse." sighed Carter.

'Let's just walk, There's a marked trail. We can't stay the night here." said Ella.

They started walking down the path. A long, cold, dark, seemingly never-ending path. It all seemed to be fine for an hour, but that's when they heard the same rustling noises from the nearby bushes and shrubs.

Alerted, their pace of walking increased. They huddled close. Despite the arguments, they were very close to each other.

THE WESARKHS.

A high pitched bang. Before any of them knew it, they were blindfolded, in a second, unconscious.

"Where are we?" said Ella as she gained consciousness. She was the first one to wake up.

She looked around. They were in a dark chamber. With a locked door. The only source of light was a ray of sunlight peeking through a crack in the stone wall.

"What the hell! Carter! Veronica! Noah! Paris! Oliver! Wake up!" she panicked.

Soon after, the other five gained consciousness as well.

"Where are we?"

"This just keeps getting worse."

"We're all gonna die."

"Stop it. We've clearly been kidnapped. Not murdered. We're alive guys. We'll survive." said Carter in a hope to ignite a fire of survival in his friends.

"Really, we're basically dead. Kidnapped by a bunch of people dressed in animal skin in the middle of a forest."

The door suddenly opened. And there they saw a man, dressed in the same attire as the ones they saw before. He was carrying a wood axe with the, beside him stood a woman with the same attire.

"Get up," said the woman.

"You speak English, thank god. Please get us out of here. We're good people with families. We just want to go home." said Paris.

Before they could say anything more, they were forced outside the chamber and dragged to a huge chamber, Well lit with candles and fires. There sat a man on a wooden chair. He seemed to be their leader.

"Good people. You said. The person you killed in the forest was a good person too! He had a family. He wanted to live. But you killed him. You must pay" said the woman.

"He would've killed us! He was threatening us! It was self-defence>"

"Self defence? He merely wanted to help you city people get out of the forest before it got too dark. You don't know anything about this forest, the creatures that lure here during the night. He wanted to help you. But you killed him."

"How would have we known that he was trying to help us? He was dressed like a stone age man, he talked like a mad person."

"Judgement. You judge people like us. You think we're foolish, cruel, evil and inferior versions of you. When we're better in every way. Look around, we have no poverty, no hunger, no sorrow, no disease. Now tell me, who is the madman?"

"Enough! We have seen and heard enough. You will all be punished for your crimes. Tomorrow at dawn we will perform the Fariash. Praise to the Wesarkhs!" screamed their leader.

THE FARIAH

They were led back to the small dark chamber. Terrified and clueless, they had given up nearly all hope of surviving.

"This is it! We're all gonna die." said Paris, tears coming out of her eyes.

"This was supposed to be a weekend trip! It's become a trip to death's door instead." said Ella.

"Can't we escape?" said Oliver

"Escape? Are you crazy? We'll die if they catch us" said Ella.

"Well they're planning to kill us already, why not give life one last shot. We have nothing to lose but everything to gain." said Oliver.

"You do have a point, we're gonna die either way. It

is better to die fighting." said Carter.

"But how do we escape? We don't know anything about this forest." said Veronica.

"We just need to get out of this settlement. Rest would be fairly easy."

The group nodded in agreement. It was nearly night. They were to receive their death penalty tomorrow. They needed to move and move fast.

"Hurry up, out the ladder everyone!" said Oliver.

The group followed out the ladder. Outside the chamber they saw what anyone would believe to be a normal village in a forest. Only the group of friends knew how unusual it actually was.

"There! That's a path! It probably leads out of here. We need to be careful and discreet. Come on" said Paris pointing out to a stone path that seemingly led to the forest.

They walked the path slowly and steadily. Making no noise. Terrified of the fate that was awaiting them.

"What was that!" exclaimed Ella when they heard the bushes around them shuffling.

"Shhh, we must not panic. Do not scream Ella, you'll attract the attention of those lunatics. Let's just go" said Carter, trying to calm his sister.

They walked for miles, for hours. Equally terrified still. Fighting for their lives. It was now or never.

The sun slowly rose, and they saw the government authorised trail once again.

Were they safe? Did they survive this nightmare?

"We told you to stay in your chamber! Have you no shame? Killing one of our people and running from your deserved punishment. You're worse than animals." the Wesarkh lady said as she appeared out of the bushes. Behind her walked many more of her people, with spears and weapons of all sorts.

"Please we never meant any harm! We are sorry, we apologise. Please spare our lives."

"Finish them!" said the lady. With a cold dark expression on her face, a near sly smile.

Bam! Bam! Logs of wood hit Carter and Oliver's head. They were ripped open. Right in front of their friends.

Arrows went through Paris's body.

A sword sliced Noah's body into two halves.

Ella was set on fire.

Veronica, the only one who remained standing and alive, looked around at the sight of absolute horror in front of her. She didn't say anything. She broke down, sobbing. She was ready to die.

WHAT IF?

"Veronica! Veronica! Wake up. You're gonna be late for school!"

Veronica opened her eyes. She was lying on her bed, in her room. Her mother told her to wake up.

She couldn't understand what was happening.

"Where am I?' she said with a trembling voice.

"Sweet, you're in your house, of course. Are you okay? Did you have a nightmare?"

Veronica didn't reply.

"Well, let it be. You have school and the camping night you have planned with your friends! Ella and Carter called to tell me all about it. Sounds fun! Come on down for breakfast and hurry up." said Veronica's mother as she left the room.

Veronica was alive? Carter and Ella were alive? Was it all a nightmare?

They're going on a camping trip today? What if?

And the rest was a story for another day.

Chapter 15

Dance To My Heartbeat

Tia Choudhury

Two years ago, had I not made that promise, I wouldn't be here today. I'd still be sitting in my house, bored, with nothing to bring life into me, trying to survive the grind of college. That promise was what made me who I am.

It was the first year of college, and our parents had bought us a small apartment to share. Riley and I were born to rich homes and were best friends since childhood. Each of our parents had worked hard to get the life they had, and they insisted we do the same. They didn't spoil us but didn't stop themselves from spoon feeding us every one of life's luxuries either. Almost half of the first semester had ended when Riley asked me, "Brooke, why have you been behaving so oddly ever since we started college?"

I said nothing. "If there's something wrong, just tell me," Riley said, calmly. "I don't know," I replied, "nothing seems fun anymore. I've got good parents, I know what I want to be, I am talented enough to be what I want to be. It's too easy."

"Isn't that a good thing? Living without any problems in your life," Riley asked.

"Life isn't fun when you don't have problems to deal with," I said. I guessed Riley agreed with me on that, because there was an awkward silence in the room. "I'll think about it then. If I get a solution I'll tell you. Just take care of yourself bro," Riley said, and went to bed.

A few days had passed, but we still hadn't got a cure to this 'illness of sorts' I had. I was heading to my fine arts class when I saw a girl handing out flyers. She gave me one and said, "Please participate if you love dancing."

I did love dancing. I wanted to become a dance teacher, and I'd teach contemporary dance. The flyer that advertised an inter-college dance competition gave me a good opportunity. But was this what I needed?

I showed the flyer to Riley as soon as we returned from our part-time jobs. Her happiness seemed to explode when she read it. "This is what you need, my friend! This is your cure," she screamed. "You need to participate in this thing!"

"Ok, if you say so…" I said. I was still uncertain about whether I should take the step or not. But Riley would not stop trying to convince me, so I said yes just to shut her up.

The next day, I went to the dance studio of

my college to talk to competition. I supposed major Coone about the inquiring about the event, bunts would be there was only one. from me, there

Daniel was a year above me. H interest in dancing, and he too was du the lack of students interested in the eve a great Coone briefed us about the competition. by make our own dance routine in our own catego prepare for the show in about three months.

I immediately started working on the routine once I got home. The challenge was accepted.

The next few months would prove to be the busiest months of all my life. Squishing the dance practice into my already full schedule wasn't easy. I often went to the dance studio to practice and found Daniel there. As I watched, it became clear that Daniel was far more skilled at dancing than I was.

Dancing had consumed his entire life. I felt a pressure within myself to practice more and match his level.

However, slowly, I got better and better at dancing. This was the first time I really had to struggle with anything. When I heard Professor Coone praise my dancing more, my heart felt full. The first round of the contest was getting closer and I was getting more nervous. Riley and Daniel were able to calm me just a

few days before th...ere, I waited. I heard my name
Contest d... ...nt up to the stage. I liked to think
...rm of magic, because I went into a
being call... ...rformed, and didn't feel for a second that
of i... ...housand people were watching me perform.
...rformance ended and I went backstage.

I didn't know how I had performed until Professor ...oone called us to the dance studio. "You danced like an angel," he said, "I'm so proud of both of you."

Daniel bagged first position in his category (which was freestyle), and I won second in mine. I didn't win in my category, but I felt more alive than ever.

The second round would have the top three dancers of every category competing. All the qualifiers would compete against everyone else. That meant Daniel was my competition. I worked harder than ever to be better than he was. I included newer, more complex moves to make my choreography look unique. I'd often ask Riley to review my dances, in case she'd be of any help.

I was spending almost half of my days doing dance practice those days, even dancing around at my part time job to keep my creativity up and running. Days were flashing by and the competition was drawing closer. About a week before the main event, the organisers invited the participants to a gathering for a cool down.

Riley dropped me off to the venue that day. I realised I didn't know anyone as I entered the hall. I knew no one there. Luckily, I saw Daniel sitting at the bar table, waving at me. "How's practice going," He asked. "Stressful," I replied, "I'd rather spend this time practicing."

"You're worrying too much. I've seen great choreographers mess up on stage because they panicked too much," Daniel said. I agreed silently.

"But why aren't you nervous?"

Daniel sighed.

After a moment, he said, "I am nervous, but I know as long as I love dancing, I won't mind not winning a contest." "What do you mean," I asked.

"You remember how you told me your heart felt full even when you didn't win in the first round?"

"Yes!"

"It's the same feeling, I won't mind getting second or third place. There will always be room for improvement, but I'll be happy as long as I'm satisfied. That's what matters," he said.

I felt good to be on the same page as him that day. I calmed down.

In the blink of an eye, the event day had come. I managed to keep my confidence up while still being mesmerised by the other participants' performances. My name got called, and I was on stage once again. The music started playing, and I started dancing. The magic that had worked the first time returned.

I was flowing on stage, like a fish in water. The eyes of the thousands of viewers didn't phase me at all. I finished my performance, bowed one last time, and went backstage again. I didn't realise how much I enjoyed that day till the event had ended.

***

My stomach lurched as I walked toward the dance studio. The results for the competition had arrived and I was more nervous than ever. I entered the room. Daniel and Professor Coone were already there.

The expression on Professor's face wasn't grim, but it was enough to make my stomach lurch even more. "We didn't win the competition," he said. Daniel and I looked at each other, and I knew what we were feeling was the same. "But," Professor Coone suddenly said, "We are in the top three winners of the contest."

The smile on our faces returned. "What is the exact lineup," Daniel asked. "Well, you two only have a difference of one point," Professor said. "Who got the one point," I asked.

He made us wait. After a long silence, the Professor finally said, "Brooke got the point. She got second and you third, Daniel."

I was on cloud nine. Daniel reached his hand out and said, "Congratulations."

I shook his hand and congratulated him as well. I might not have one, but like last time, my heart was full.

After some time professor Coone took our attention and said, "You two are great dancers and even better students. Now, promise me you both will never miss a chance at an opportunity like this one."

Daniel nodded. Professor looked at me. I nodded too and said, "I promise."

Chapter 16

The night I lost

Jyotsna Bisht

I looked out the window, and snow gathered on the footsteps. But my mind trails on a different path, a party with a big ballroom. Rich people in their fanciest and ridiculous gowns floating around, telling stories of golf. ' Two kids down the hallway run for the exit after setting fire to babysitter's wig for stealing their cookies, which I now look back and think wasn't the best way to serve justice but little did our tiny minds know, for us it was just sweet revenge. Down our parents panicked to the worries of fire, where up above we forgot the city lights in the glistening twilight. I remember, you looked at me, your eyes glimmering under moon and said "pinky promise, never to leave me?" I looked at you with confusion running in my head but I didn't take the question because my answer has always been yes, then why did yours change?' I question the lifeless body of her, in front of me. The sound of a flat line leaves everyone in a deep dead cold except me, the only thing running through my brain is the flames of fury. Lightening my every never, I take the flower vase from the side and crash it into the window. The doctor and the nurses tried to calm me but logical thinking was something lacking in my mind as chaos spread followed by destruction and disarray, I threw all of the objects on the ground. Soon security comes to escort me to safety, which is to the psychic ward. "I'M NOT CRAZY, LET ME OUT" shouts continued until I woke up completely dizzy with my hands tied and a doctor examining me like a rare species of wild boar. He started speaking, which only made the matters worse, as now my anger is also fueled by their horrid treatment of a person grieving with trauma. I shouted slurs at him, which to my surprise didn't work but as I started regaining consciousness, I realized if I want to get out of here, I need to be on my best behavior and at least pretend I'm fine. I took a deep sigh and apologized, he asked me a few things and wanted me to discuss my "feelings' ' as in the aggressive behavior to which I started to act out a whole sob story. I'm distressed by her death but I'm concerned with giving the same fate as hers to the one who caused this. I have to be the one to solve this because I know her parents are just going to feed the hospital and the police money to cover this up as an "accident". Their daughter died but god knows, they are more concerned over their reputation which not now but later will be ruined by their own blood, but that's a tale for later. Luckily he bought into my life as I slid past our families crying the tears of a crocodile.

I got to my car when I noticed her husband's car wasn't there. I know they didn't have the best relationship but I really expected him to be there. James is not just her husband but he's his best friend. He was there for her when even her whole family decided to disown her, he's not going to leave her like that, plus for an event like this it's expected of him to appear for the press. If James isn't here then where is he? I know the cleanup and coverage is never done by a spouse. And I know there can be no office work because the buyers return on Thursday and the shipment isn't for another week. After a few moments of theorizing I shake my head to realize he's probably at home sobbing with grief as none of the people here seems to know about it and I may find some clue.

The moment I reach there, something is wrong. I find blood dripped fingertips on his car door, I gasp as I fall back at the sight of it. I know she suspected he might be having an affair but I can't believe it would get this far. He's known her since childhood, we used to play together, mess with the royals and pull pranks on the upper class, and we were best friends. No I might be wrong he would not betray her, no betray us like this, there must be another explanation I'm sure. My shaky hand turns to open the gates to find more evidence, hopefully he's not in the living room from what I can tell. Bless the technology, it's so easy to hack into, can't imagine if it was a traditional lock. I quickly scan the rooms for a slight mistake but all I'm met with is disappointment until I hear the footsteps. Oh no, he's coming, I quickly run into the attic to hide but the moment I open the door I'm met with a fishy smell, coming from a bag stained red. Tears stream down my eyes but without a second thought I call the cops and my family as my heart beat rises I open the bag to find broken glass with blood as if someone crashed it into the skull. I scream abruptly, alerting my presence to him, luckily the sirens come into view but too late as he sneaks up behind me and smashes my head into the rusty table lying nearby. That's all I remember as the world slowly comes into view as I look around me to realize I'm in the hospital bed but without the shackles this time, that's a good thing. I touch my head to realize there is surgical tape, a hurting wound and my missing hair. The family gathers around asking me several questions but as I grow more aware of my surroundings I start to realize all the events that happened today. I lost two people, the only two people who ever truly knew me.

Chapter 17

TRUTH AND HONESTY

Aarya Shankar

Long, long ago….the time of when you couldn't even think of your existence. Oh! I mean even Adam and Eve couldn't have thought of their existence, there, up in the sky were hanging a family of nine. Now, you shouldn't be astonished when I tell you that you're perfectly aware of who they were; none other than the solar family! Which comprised of little boys Mercury and Venus, father Mars, grandpa Jupiter, the fashionable daughter Saturn, the generous of all mother Earth and the two useless distant relatives who interfered in every matter, Uranus and Neptune. And yes! How can I forget the adopted baby Pluto who'd a special place in his frozen heart for growing up.

God once came to them and indulged them in the task of forming life on themselves. He said, "Whoever from all nine of you will find success in the task of creating lives on themselves will get humans as a reward."

All the planets geared up themselves and set off in completion of the task. They took help from the rains, asked for a favour to the air, knocked on the hot door of the Sun and did all they could. But well what was the result finally? I'm pretty sure that you know what happened next however, I can't resist myself from telling you that mother Earth was the only one who fulfilled the task by adding the right measures of atmosphere, just a bit of help from the sun and a few requests from the rains to be able to fill the seas and the rivers. She'd green plants, patterned insects and all sorts of beautiful animals all around! She informed all the family members about the same. Father Mars and grandpa Jupiter were expressionless as always. Little boys Mercury and Venus were hopping around on their orbits, happy for their mother's success. Distant relatives Uranus and Neptune were jealous as ever. However, Pluto remained expressionless.

After the completion of such a daunting task, Earth went to sleep. Taking advantage, Pluto sent a few of his rocks towards Earth to quietly pick up a few of the most lively and appealing creatures.

Finally the day came. God asked, "Did any of you all attain success?" Earth said, "Oh! Great God, By your blessings I was able to produce life for myself."

Just then Pluto sighted his rocks coming and they safely delivered the theft to him. Pluto then shouted, "Oh God, I've done the same too!" Everybody, including God, was surprised. God went closer to him and found that all the creatures on freezing Pluto were on the verge of dying.

God knew it all now. He was furious. He scolded Pluto for being so very dishonest and untruthful.

He even cursed Pluto for becoming smaller than ever. He was disowned from the solar family and was even teased by the name 'dwarf'. Earth was rewarded with humans.

So well, dear reader, now you know that why there are only eight planets in the solar

system and why your boring textbook told you to learn dishonest Pluto's name as 'dwarf'.

Chapter 18

SLAPPY: THE REVENGE OF THE DEVIL DUMMY

Vidisha Saxena

Sera Stine is unwillingly moving from New York City to Madison. Arriving at the new house, she is greeted by the neighbor, the family of a mother, and her son named Dak. Sera's father, Dr. Ed Stine gruffly tells him to stay on his side of the fence. The next evening when Dak is taking out the garbage, sera walks up and startles him. He asks her to take a walk with him, and he leads her into a forest. They arrive at an abandoned park, and they climb up to the top of a Ferris wheel. Sera says that she has never met her mother and dak tells her that his father has abandoned him. Back on the ground, they walk home, and Sera's dad grabs her shoulder and orders her back inside. After a week, dak decided to sneak into sera's house to see if she was fine. He went through the kitchen window and he saw a button, which he pressed to switch on the light; as soon as he did so, he fell into a library. Dak screamed. The scream made sera rush downstairs; she was amazed to see a library in the kitchen. Dak saw an old chest and opened it, he saw a red book inside and unlocked it. Just then sera saw a Huge shadowy figure swinging a baseball bat at Dak's head. Before she could even think about the figure, a fifteen-foot snowman appeared, bounding out through a wall and running off into the forest. Sera runs after the monster, with Dak running after. Following the trail of destruction, He arrives at an ice rink. He sees Sera climb in through a broken window, and He follows. He walks out to her, and gummy bear candy rains down around them. Sera had no idea about what was going on.

As the monster runs toward her, she opens the book and the monster starts to get sucked in, but then it lifts its arm and swats the book out of her hands. Sera understands that she needs to suck the monster inside the book and runs toward the book, but the monster slams his fist down. Dr. Ed shows up and opens the book, and the monster gets sucked in. He shuts the book and orders them into the car. After reaching home, Dak goads Dr. Ed to reveal his true identity. Dr. Ed tells him that as a child, he had the habit of staying indoors and the neighborhood kids would taunt him. He made up monsters to spend time with, and one day they became real, leaping off the page. He says they're safe as long as the books stay locked, Dak finds "Slappy The Devil Dummy" on the floor with a broken lock.

They hear a burst of evil laughter, Dr. Ed approaches

Slappy with the book, but Slappy sets the pages on fire. Slappy leaves the house with another book from the chest. They drive around town looking for Slappy, finding only destruction everywhere. Dr. Ed rushes to the school to grab his typewriter because he knows that now he needs to write another book. Sera and Dak rush to the nearby store, to hide. They see a wolf gnawing on a steak. They try to sneak by, but the wolf hears them and starts running their way. Dak distracts the wolf to escape. The wolf sees them and resumes the chase. The wolf breaks down the door, and the group finds themselves trapped in the back parking lot, with the wolf rapidly closing the distance. Suddenly, a car rams the wolf, knocking it into a brick wall.

At the school, they heave a sigh of relief that the tiny robots with laser eyes break through and twelve-foot scarecrows punch holes in the windows, Dr. Ed furiously types out a story, and Slappy approaches. Slappy says that if he stops, Slappy will let him live. When he refuses, Slappy slams the lid on his hands, breaking his fingers. Dr. Ed Dictated what to write. Ed knows that Slappy will find him wherever he goes since they share thoughts. They all hide in the funhouse in the abandoned amusement park, Slappy finds them and unleashes the last monster, Glob-Blob. They all climb up the Ferris wheel as the Blob eats Ed with one gulp.

Sera cries out, but she sees that he's still alive inside the body. Dr. Ed revealed that sera is fiction. When he locked the monsters inside the book he created, Sera, dearest to him, Ed orders Dak to write that, sera being a part of the story vanishes inside the book. Sera started to fade with teary eyes. As the Blob gets dragged along, Ed is able to free himself, but Slappy grabs onto him, trying not to fall into the book. Ed kicks Slappy into the book, Dak shuts it, and the wind dies down. Months later, the town is rebuilt, the school reopens, and Dr. Ed is now an English professor in the school. Later, he finds his typewriter and sees the keys move on their own, and on the paper appears, "The Invisible Boy's Revenge." He just remembered that he forgot to mention the invisible boy in the story! He sees his scared reflection in a glass window, and next to it, a tiny hand print.

Chapter 19

Good Bye

Vani Sharma

"The Story never starts and ends
The way you think it should be.."

I just think that everyone should have the potential to do anything they want to do and not just drag themselves into the things they know they will never do, I mean just why do the things you don't have the ability to?

Allow me to introduce myself. I'm Nerreza Davies, a 20-year-old woman who prefers observation over conversation. Unfortunately, I'm growing weary of a certain habit that many people possess.

Tomorrow, I must make it to my art school. It's not a matter of giving up; I've been struggling for a year now, and the toll is catching up to me. Only I know how much humiliation and failure I've faced. Recovering from it all hasn't been easy, but I haven't been alone in this journey.

My parents? They don't exist in this world. I remember the day vividly when they dropped me off at school on December 6, 2009. It was a Monday, and the time was 7:33 A.M. Little did I know it would be the last time I would bid them farewell. They were involved in a car accident shortly after dropping me off, and I cried for hours that day.

Oddly enough, I've always had a fondness for rain. However, since that fateful day, whenever it rains, the memories of that tragic event come flooding back, making the day unbearable for me.

NEXT DAY

This is my final try, I hope I do my best or else...

"Okay Students, The results are-

1st Position Michelle

2nd Position Falek

3rd Position Kristy

and Nerreza, I wish you could make it but it's okay, try one more time." said the teacher.

"No teacher, I won't do it another time. Thank you for supporting me every time. I'll get going. Goodbye."

I will just do any other thing, and I'll succeed in it. It's Okay.

I have to clean my room, though.

What is this? Oh, I used to write songs in high school. How nice.

Hey, should I try it one more time?

Days I went through when you were not there
when I had no one beside me to wipe my tears.
At the time I had no idea where to go,
I wandered in the dark alleys,
having thoughts to kill me.
I still showed up to everyone
that my life was something nice and I was a cheerful
person when I was not that. Right?
Having no goals, no map to life.
I trembled my path a thousand times.
Things I did not do right...
I still showed up to everyone
that my life was something nice and I was a cheerful
person when I was not that. Right?
I didn't know who I am for months
What do you think it just seems like?
No one noticed the change in me,
and I did hold it up. Right?
I still showed up to everyone
that my life was something nice and I was a cheerful
person when I was not that. Right?

WOAH, I didn't know I would just continue with this as my career too...

Can I just post these on social media, No no? Should I just improve or make it nicer??

The songs which could just connect to the feelings of listeners?

Hey! It's so great!!

Good Job Nerreza! Good Job!!

Let me make more...

NEXT DAY

Today I have to go by bus...oh How exhausting...

Raining, Raining
My loved ones draining draining in blood,
and I am just straining straining to pain,
No, the time never got easier but I just got harder.
We bid our last goodbyes seeing each other's eyes.
Those eyes were smiling, one second passed and they were crying,
What thing could be so bad that did hurt me?
My world was visible in your eyes,
Did it end right away?
I hope I could never be the one writing this but it had me through all my pasts, even when we all laughed, cheered, and smiled and I could never forget that.
We bid our last goodbyes seeing each other's eyes.
Those eyes were smiling, one second passed and they were crying,
What thing could be so bad that did hurt me?
Maybe, you were never going to live with me,

but I hope you are happy~
I see you in the sky every time you look beautiful
Heaven made you smile more...
We bid our last goodbyes seeing each other's eyes...

I wrote it sitting on the window seat and one guy recorded this and I didn't even notice. I just got a notification from Instagram... The comments are really nice.

"Hey, You are really good, why don't you sing in movies?"

"Did you write it? Daebak. That's so great!"

"I would love to hear your voice all day If I'd get a chance. You are so good!!"

That made me smile.

Human Nature tends to be attracted to things and just thinking they would do it even when they have something really special that no one could ever have in them itself. Sometimes it's really important to just take a glance at your past and walk by the memories,

Maybe you are not made up for the present and your past can make your future.

Even though it sometimes feels like doing what you are doing right now, there's nothing bad if you just remember your past and build up your future.

Chapter 20

THE PERFECT SCAR

Shreya Srivastava

A girl named Irene lived with her brother Jack peacefully until one day… She was roaming around in the streets. Suddenly she tripped over a stone and fell in a river nearby. She saw a beautiful twinkling star before everything went blank.

When she got her senses back, she was in a room of a palace. Thousands of questions roamed around her mind. The first person she saw was a young lady standing happily as you opened your eyes. She was calling her "princess" and asking how she fell in the river. Irene replied that I don't know you or this place. Everyone including The King was telling her very unfamiliar things. When the king told the year is 502, she was extremely shocked. The doctor who came to check her told Irene may have lost her memories but deep down she knew she was not the one they were talking about.

In these few days, she got to know many things about the real princess. She looked exactly like her. Until one day her court lady told that she had a "perfect scar" on her back. Later that night she hesitantly checked if the scar was there or not. This was the only way to find out that her soul went into the princess body or she time traveled. To her surprise it was not there...

One day, she went into a library nearby. Her eyes fell on a book named The Magical Star. She found out this was the star she saw that night before falling. It was the princess's star. Why did she saw this? Why did she come here?

She was walking on the road until a stranger approached her. He whispered "I know you are not the real princess". She was shocked and asked how he knew this. But the next thing gave her answers to all her questions...

The day she fell was the day the king's best friend pushed the princess in the river. Princess saw the star and wished that someone would take her place and save the kingdom. And that's how she came here. "Save the kingdom?" asked Irene.

The stranger said that the king's best friend wanted to take this throne by killing him. The stranger was an astrologer. He told that she would return back if she went to the same river by tomorrow morning. Irene made her decision to save the kingdom.

The next day, King introduced someone as his best friend. She was shocked to see it was her present-life brother. Before she could say anything, the king pulled her and checked the scar. The king was burning with anger while his friend was enjoying it. She tried to tell him everything but how would he believe an unknown person over his best friend. He expelled her out of the palace…

Later that night, his best friend came to her and said "you were lucky you got saved that day, but not now" and went. On the other hand, the king was missing you. He kind of liked your company but was angry that you lied to him about your identity. The same astrologer came to him and told him everything. Tears were falling from his eyes. He believed his best friend but look what he did. He attacked his kingdom the very next day. Both their armies were killed. Jack was about to stab him but Irene came out of nowhere and back stabbed him. King was so happy to see her. He asked for her apology and decided to make her his real princess. Every obstacle was removed from their life. They lived happily ever after…

Chapter 21

The Mystery Maze

Akshansh Gupta

Have you ever been trapped in an underground maze, filled with mythological creatures?

"Well here I am"

So allow me to introduce myself and my fellow travellers. Atlas Damon is my name, and I'm 19 years old. I travelled to Egypt with my friends Steve Castle and Diana Grace to investigate the enigmatic Giza Pyramids.

You're probably wondering how a group of young teens ended up in a death maze at this point.

So It all started when we were exploring the pyramids of Giza, or at least two of us were exploring. Steve was trying to find treasure with his Dowsing L Rods. Steve then informed us that there was a wooden gate in one of the toes of the Great Sphinx and a bright light was shining behind it

Now despite all the possibly true rumours about traps in pyramids, who chose to go in.

There was a strange odour inside. We pulled our torches out and started walking. Steve was so much focused on the L rods that he didn't appear to care about the fact that there were skulls and bones on the ground. Diana was afraid, though.

We approached a descending stairway as we continued to walk on. We arrived at the bottom of the stairs after about 20 minutes. At the bottom there appeared to be a tiny ancient city at the bottom. A large structure, which appeared to be a temple, was present in the centre of the city. Now, despite the fact that we were incredibly underground, it felt colder than outside. We made our way to the temple. As we drew closer to the temple, Steve became more and more thrilled as it appeared that the L rods were showing more and more m0vement. On the walls of the temple's interior, there were stone paintings facing the other way. The paintings on the left side resembled the Egyptian God of Sun Ra, while the images on the right side resembled the Egyptian God of Moon Khonshu. We started exploring the temple. Diana found a Gold coin lying on the floor of the temple so she decided to keep it as a souvenir. Steve told us to move towards the small room because according to his L rods, there was treasure in it. He was going Frenzy about it. We moved to the small room and just as we entered the doors of the room closed. Inside the room there were four old animal statues similar to those you may buy in a pricey gift shop kept on a stone table. The figures resembled dragon, hawk, fish and a hippopotamus. There were also 4 pillars in each corner of the room with a hole in them such that to fit one of the figures in them. Each pillar represented Earth, Sky, Water and Fire. It occurred to Diana that we had to place the figures in the pillars according to the element they represented. I placed the dragon in the fire pillar, Steve placed the fish in the water pillar and the hippopotamus in the Earth pillar and Diana placed the Hawn in the Sky pillar.

Now I don't remember much but of what I could make out, it appeared that we had travelled back in time. We were in the same room but now instead of being all dusty and spooky, it was bright red and seemed to be well maintained. The gates were now open and we all rushed out.

It seemed like a whole new world now, all green and beautiful, fresh air, calm and blue water and large trees. Steve was sad and disappointed for not finding the treasure but Diana was amused.

Chapter 22

FOLLOW YOUR DREAMS

Ahana Singh

Once upon a time, there was a family of Leafmen. They had a very talented son named Sam, who was a great musician with a melodious voice. However, his parents wanted him to work for the lion's palace as it was a government job and would bring in a lot of money. Sam, on the other hand, was passionate about music and wanted to become a famous singer.

One day, as he was whispering to himself about his dreams, his mother overheard him and yelled, "No, you will work for the government and bring us a lot of money." His father added, "Your mother is right. You can't follow your dreams if you don't have money."

Sam refused to give up on his dream and said, "I want to follow my dreams, and if it's about money, I will earn it by singing."

His parents disagreed and shouted, "No, you won't!"

Sam was heartbroken and went to his room to cry. To his surprise, his guitar started talking to him. "I have been alive since your childhood," the guitar said. "I have watched you and think you are great at what you do. If you listen to me, you can achieve your dreams."

Sam was amazed and asked the guitar, "What should I do?"

The guitar replied, "Sing as much as you want. Sing for the trees and the plants in the forest. Sing for the animals. You have to struggle to achieve success, but I believe in you."

Sam agreed and started singing in the forest. He sang for the trees, the plants, and the animals. He worked hard and eventually got the opportunity to sing for the King Lion.

He sang a beautiful song with his guitar, and the King was so impressed that he made Sam the chief of all singers and musicians in the jungle.

Sam's fame grew, and he started singing for humans, becoming famous all over the world. He remained humble and kind, even with his success.

His parents saw him on big stages and realized their mistake. Sam visited them one day, and they admitted their mistake. Sam forgave them, and they all lived happily ever after.

Chapter 23

Fortunately Misfortuned

Dhruvika Madhesia

Silence.

That was the only thing that was heard. As I dropped myself on my bed, staring at the ceiling thinking about my life.

The regular nine-to-five job, orders from managers, and complete darkness.

I lazily got up from my bed, freshened up, and went to my bed again.

Early this morning, I woke up to the sound of the alarm clock ringing and my phone pinging with notifications. I checked my phone only to find that I'm running late. I hurriedly dressed and left for my workplace.

As I reached there, we met our manager standing at my table, looking furious. After listening to a lot of lectures, I sighed and sat in my place, getting ready to face eight hours of emotional and physical damage. I didn't know how fast the time flew as I checked the clock showing 8:30 pm. I packed my things and got out.

The streets were beautifully decorated with orange Chinese Lanterns. The time of Chinese New Year is my favorite, the only time that makes me happy. Since I didn't have my dinner, I went down the street to my favourite Chinese restaurant. I have been visiting this place since the time I have been here in Boston. As I entered inside, the addicting aroma of dumplings filled my nostrils. I greeted the old lady who owns this restaurant. She always used to greet back with a smile but she didn't do that today, she had a rather concerned look on her face. Weird. Ignoring that, I sat on the table next to the window admiring how gorgeous the streets looked. After having my food, as I was getting up to pay, a waiter came up to me. He gave me a box and said they're giving gift boxes to all the customers due to the Chinese New Year. I thanked him and left the place.

I reached my apartment, dropped my things on the couch, and opened the gift box. As I opened it, it turned out to be a fortune cookie. Pretty cheap for a New year's gift. Anyway, I opened the cookie and found a paper chit inside of it. I ate the cookie and opened the chit to see my "fortune". "Your life is in danger. Don't tell this to anyone. Leave the city and run far far away. Repeat: Don't tell this to anybody." I was dumbfounded but then burst into fits of laughs. I mean this is a pretty good prank for April Fools' day.

Throwing that chit in the trashcan, I went towards the refrigerator to grab a bottle of water. Chugging the water down my throat I went to bed. As I was scrolling through social media, a notification popped up on my device. It was a text from an unknown number. As I opened the text, it read the same message as in the chit I just threw. Weird. As I was lost in my thoughts, another message pinged up on the screen. "I knew you wouldn't believe me. Now go and pick up that chit from the dustbin again". Okay, how in the actual Hogwarts do they know I threw the chit in the dustbin!! I went to the kitchen and picked up that chit from the dustbin again. By the time I was observing it, another message came up on my phone- "Believe me or not, this is true." I turned the chit around but it had nothing except a watermark of a bird, a black cuckoo.

I spent the night just thinking about the chit, that unknown number and the black cuckoo watermark. The next morning I woke up with dark eyebags around my eyes. I went to my workplace as usual but my thoughts were revolving around that unknown number and that chit all the time.

After my office hours, I hurriedly packed up my things and ran to the restaurant where I got that fortune cookie from. As I reached that place, I was met with a signboard which said that this place would be closed for the upcoming month due to the occasion of the New Year. I was going to leave that place, but just that moment something caught my eye. A black cuckoo watermark. The same black cuckoo watermark.

Just as I was going to touch it, a pamphlet fell from somewhere. It was an advertising pamphlet for the new hotel the Black Bird industries opened in our area. Wait. The logo of Black Bird industries is a Black Cuckoo. The same Black Cuckoo. Why didn't I notice this before? I ran towards my home with the pamphlet in my hand. I quickly threw my things on the couch and opened my laptop. I searched for the Black Bird group on the internet and found something weird. I read an article which said that the Owner of Blackbird industries is anonymous. I jumped in happiness as this news is going to solve all the mysteries. But then I realized how I am going to find out the owner of blackbird industries.

I read a lot of articles the whole night, jotting down all the important things I found on the internet.

The next morning, I didn't go to my workplace, instead, I visited the headquarters of Blackbird Industries. The building was way too tall to fit in my sight. The building's interior was beautifully decorated with white marble and the ogo of the industry on the walls. As I walked further, the receptionist came up to me and said," May I help you, sir?" I replied," Hello, is there any chance that I can meet the CEO for a minute or two?" I tried to convince her but he refused. Then an idea clicked in my mind- I took the paper chit out from my bag which was there in the fortune cookie. As her eyes landed on that paper chit, she told me to follow her.

The receptionist took me to the elevator and pressed the button for the 20th floor. The light beeped as we reached the floor.

As I stepped out, the receptionist took me to a room. A dark black room with possibly zero vision. A beam of light focused on me as I was trying hard to open my eyes. I turned around only to see the receptionist had vanished. Okay now, this is getting creepy. Just as I was pondering over the situation a voice echoed in the empty room. "Hello, Chen Haitao." I looked around to see the owner of the voice. It was a tall, well-built man, looking not a day older than 32. He was staring right at me with a cold, dark expression. I was already really scared and the man's gaze was making the situation worse.

"Who are you?" I hesitantly asked. "Oh, I forgot to introduce myself, apologies for that, I am James Rogers, Founder and CEO of the Black Bird Industries." Oh, so he's the owner of the group. This guy looks kind of friendly though. "First things first, why am I here?" I said."Oh yes, this is important, I run a mission which saves the lives of animals in times of distress. So you have been chosen for that." I was dumbfounded by his statements. I mean, I researched about the whole mysterious chit thing, came here to meet the CEO and he's saying that I have been selected for an animal saving mission! "So what's with that fortune cookie thing?" I questioned. Oh, that was just for your curiosity about the mission. Anyways, the details of the mission will reach you by today. Till then you may leave." I looked at him in disbelief as I walked outside the room. I mean I did all this hard work, and took a leave from the workplace, only to be known that I'm chosen for an animal mission?

Chapter 24

Adventure to the magical world

Adamya Singh

CHAPTER – 1 THE MAGICAL PAPER

Once upon a time, there was a boy named Charles. He was seventeen years old and was born in Canada. He loved adventures, hunting, and camping. One day he was coming home late because of extra classes at school. On his way, there was a raw road he was walking carefully but accidentally he stumbled on a rock his knee got cut but he stood and his eyes got attention to a piece of paper. He picked up the paper it was a strange paper but nothing was written on it but he took the paper with him.

After a few days he was looking at the paper he thought that the paper was magical but these things are not in real life he said and kept the paper in his bag. After a few days when he was coming home he again thought about the paper he again took it out and thought about it and after a few seconds suddenly the lights shuts off. Charles goes out to check the electricity. He saw that the electric wires were not working his parents called the electricians they said that it will take them 15 minutes to repair it, Charles went to his room. He noticed that the paper was glowing he was scared for a moment but he checked the paper. The paper is magical, it was glowing in the dark. He noticed some text was written on it. "It is a portal in a castle. I don't know where it is in the forest but the world is magical. I am stuck here HELP Me". He got terrified while he was reading the paper. He thought that someone is pranking him but to confirm he told everything to his friends. His friends laughed at him saying "these things do not grow up dude" but one of his friends Carl who also liked the same things said I think it could be real. He asked Charles to come with him to his elder brother's (jimmy) house who loves to research these things. Hey! Brother, please help us.

What happened guys said jimmy. Charles found a paper he is saying is magical and some text is written on it about a portal in a castle and a magical world. Jimmy was also shocked while reading the paper. He said it can be real, I have to find some clues that I need some days. They all started researching, finding clues, gathering books and asking people to read the past articles and finally, they got it. A reporter named John and his friends went to a castle in Amos and never returned. It has been 16 years since they have gone there, said jimmy. Charles said so let's solve the mystery. Carl said are you crazy? It is in a castle covered by a large forest with many challenges, dangerous animals, and insects. It is not easy and the castle is also full of traps never to think of going there.

CHAPTER – 2 THE ADVENTURE

Charles was very curious about the portal in the castle. He wanted to go there but his friends warned him and as he was in college he had no time. After some weeks summer holidays were starting so he planned to solve the mystery and go to the castle. One day early in the morning while his parents were sleeping. He packed his bags geared up and left the house. He thought to take Carl and his elder brother with him but they refused to go though he wrote a letter and threw it in Carl's room through a window and then walked away to the forest and after 2 days he reached the forest.

Near the forest, there was a river flowing. He went to the river to get some water. When he was filling his water bottle due to the wind his magical paper came out of his bags and got into the river. He furiously grabbed the paper, and to his shock, on the other side of the paper, a map appeared. The map showed the directions to reach the castle. He did not waste any time and ran into the forest.

After traveling for 1 hour, he got tired and sat near a tree. He takes his water bottle to drink and while drinking he hears a weird noise. He got scared, for protection he climbed the tree near him and after a few seconds, a tiger came out of the bushes. He got more scared for some time, he sat on the tree for some while but the tiger was not going from there so he decided to make a trap. He checked his bag and he got a rope and a poisonous dart so he made a net out of the rope and tied it on the tree's branch then he got down to lure the tiger to fall into his trap.

The tiger saw him and ran to attack Charles. The tiger stuck in his net and then he threw the poisonous dart toward the tiger and in a few seconds, the tiger died after a few seconds. He killed the tiger so he felt sorry for the tiger but he had no choice. So praying to god he resumed his adventurous journey. After traveling for a while he saw a river to reach the castle he had to cross the river.

He thought of making a boat to cross the river so he started searching and gathering wood. After getting to the woods he took out the ropes and made the boat. It was getting dark so he thought it would be dangerous to cross the river now so he took out his sleeping bag and spent his night near the river. Early in the morning, he begins to cross the river. After reaching halfway he saw something coming to him. He got terrified of alligators coming from him. They surrounded him. Charles was left with no hope the alligators started attacking his boat. Out of nowhere, a rope came to him and he saw Carl and Jimmy were there. Jimmy distracted the alligators and Charles safely crossed the river. They ran as fast as they could to get away from the river. After some time they were far away from the river. Charles asked Carl how you both crossed the river, Carl said that when the alligators were charging at you at that time we crossed the river (they continued their journey). After some time they saw the castle standing In front of the castle. They knew it was not going to be easy for them but they stepped into the castle challenging the difficulties.

CHAPTER – 3 THE CASTLE

Inside the castle they saw that the castle was in the worst condition and had a suspicious smell. When they moved forward they entered a banquet hall. The chair was broken, the pictures were in pieces and the walls were cracked. When they were exploring the hall a chandelier started to fall unluckily Carl was below it but he was saved by jimmy. Charles asked, "Is everyone ok?" Carl said 'yes'. They went up to the first floor. There was a map of the whole castle. They saw that the portal was on the third floor when they moved forward and an arrow started coming out of nowhere. They saw that there were dispensers that were throwing arrows. Jimmy asked Charles to take out the map. On the map, they said "I always guide you on your way". "It is a signboard," Jimmy said. Everyone started searching for a signboard. Carl founded it. There were some arrows on the board pointing in various directions. Carl said in the banquet hall arrows were pointing in different directions. Charles said it could be a key to stop the dispenser. When Carl did the codes the dispenser's suddenly stopped.

They quickly ran up to the second floor. On the second floor, there was some armour kept on the armour stand. When they moved forward suddenly the armour started moving toward them. Jimmy saw a place to hide. They ran towards it and closed the door. Charles asked "what is this place?" Carl said I think it is a secret cabin that the king used to hide during the attack. When Jimmy saw the map there was written: "beat the dispenser and one of the dispensers will give you a bow and arrow to fight the armour". Jimmy and Carl decide that they will distract the armour and Charles will get the bow and arrow. Charles ran to the first floor and got the bow and arrow and Carl Jimmy started distracting the armour. They fought the armour and suddenly all armour fell when they were shouted with the bow and arrow. They went to the third floor and the portal was in front of them. They were very happy, they couldn't control their tears. They stepped into the portal but they didn't know how their life would change.

Chapter 25

Will I have any adventure today?

Pihu Mishra

CHARACTERS

Jake (main character) | Gracy (Jake's mother) | Ron (Jake's friend) | Meggie (Jake's friend) | Felix (Jake's friend) | Jack (Jake's friend)

INTRODUCTION

Jake was an average student. He didn't like studying. He was just daydreaming everyday. He imagined the things which can't happen in real life. His friends were with him when he needed them and they were true friends. His friends can make him smile in just a second. Jake had a teacher Mr. Smith whom he didn't like much as Mr. Smith complained about Jake anytime he makes a mistake or does not focus on his studies. Jake's mother (Gracy) scolds him very much as Jake just runs out of the house without even telling anything.

Now let's get into the story and see what adventures Jake had......

It was again a sunny Sunday morning. Jake woke up from his sleep and thought will I have any adventure today? He went to the washroom as his mom called him out. Jake Breakfast is ready… Jake finished brushing up and went to the kitchen to eat food. While he was eating breakfast his mother asked what are your plans for today? Jake said Nothing much as there is no adventure in real life. I wonder if we could go to the island?

His mother replied NO!! Exams are near and you are not even studying and You want to go out. WE ARE NOT GOING ANYWHERE!!Go and study!!

Jake directly ran to the washroom and locked himself.No matter how much his mother called him at last all she said was…

Fine stay inside throughout the day!!

Jake was just dreaming of being on an island. How fun would it be? He wanted to experience all of this.

After some time…

Jake flushed the toilet and whoa He got into an Island but there was nothing far to far as he can see…

He walked around the island and he came a little far and saw a rabbit. He came near the rabbit and he was about to pick him up but the rabbit ran…. Jake followed him and when the rabbit stopped he saw many animals . He got shocked when a panda said –

Guyss see what a human is doing on our island? Did humans get to our island? WILL THE KILL US? *He said while being scared*

Jake said No-No-No I am not here to harm you guys I too don't know how I got here .

Bear- what do you even mean?

Jake- I mean that when I got into my washroom and I flushed the toilet I was here.

Peacock- Seems like magic happened.

Jake- I really wanted my friends here

Panda- Oh! Is it so? Hmm…Let me think…..I have an idea

Jake and other animals - what is it?

Panda- we need to find the toilet seat and flush it again maybe you get back there. Also come with your friends after that

Jake- Yeah you are right! Let's find it!!

After some time.

Panda- GUYYSS!! Over here!! I found it!

Jake-OHH wow! I will go now and take my friends here and we all will enjoy.

Bear- But Do you think that you will come back again here?

Jake – I don't know but I think I will *without letting them complete he flushed the toilet seat and got back to his home again*

Jake walked slowly while tip-toeing his toes so as not to make any sound but his mother was gone to market. After that he rushed and called all his friends. They went to a park and Jake told them everything that happened.

Gracy- Oh stop joking Jake! We all know magic is not real.

Ron- Yeah you are right Gracy.

Meggie- wait-wait Let's just ask Jake that this is a prank or this is real?

Felix- Yeah let him speak too!!

Jake- Come with me I will show you guys that MAGIC IS REAL

They all went to the washroom and flushed but nothing happened.

Ron- Jake for this stupid joke you wasted our time

Everyone- Yes! You are right! It was just a waste of time

Jake- No-No-No wait let me try again let me remember how I did it..

5 minutes later

Jake thought of the adventure to visit the island and then flushed. They all came to the island.

Animals- Woohh! You back

Jake- yeah

Felix- Ahhhhh!! Bear!! Someone help save me. I am going to diee!! Ahh

Gracy- Stop being a kid Felix

Jake- As I told you I will be back and here I am .

Bear - yeah come I will show you guys our island

Jake with his friends and animals started walking around the island and then they came to a tree and the rabbit said Guys Jump in the tree . After saying that the rabbit jumped in the tree and so with other animals . Jake and his friends also jumped in the tree and they were on another island which was full of sweets. Trees,houses, everything was made of sweets . They all started eating it and they had a lot of fun that day.

At night

Guyysss!! You see it's 9:00 o'clock and we need to go home or else our mom will scold us said Meggie .

Yeah you are right! Said Ron

Jake- ohh ok! Let's go home then.

Felix- but where is the toilet seat?

Jake- yeah where is it? We need to find it or otherwise we cannot go home.

Everyone started finding it.

After some time(9:30 p.m)

Guyss here I found it said the panda.

Jake- Gracy you go first just think that I want to go to my home.

Gracy went…

Jake- Ron Now you should go

Ron went..

Meggie and Felix went too…

Jake- Thank you guys for giving me beautiful memories here. I will remember this forever. It was my dream to come to the island once.

Rabbit- Will you not come here again?

Jake- I will for sure till then goodbye guys I will come soon.

Animals- Bye bye!

Jake went to his home and his mother asked him where were you ? Jake said I was in the washroom only you only told me to stay there for a day. His mother said ok leave and come have dinner now. While having dinner Jake thought of the day how it went with animals. Was it magic or was it just his imagination? Will He have any adventure again?

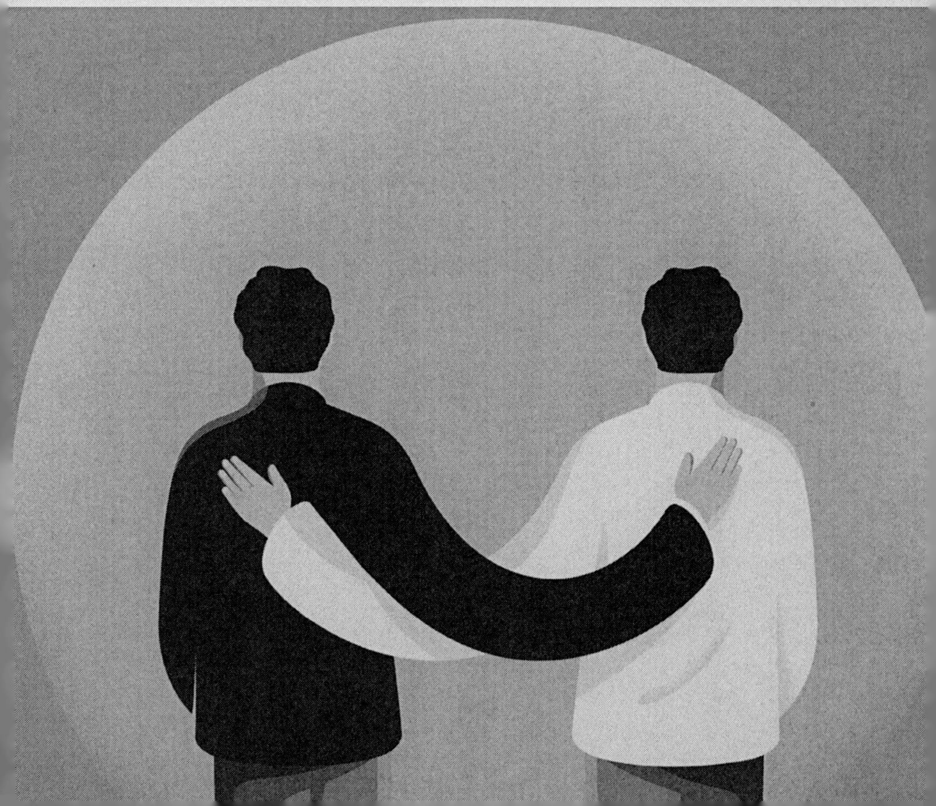

Chapter 26

Yes Serendipity

Suhani Singh

When you forget to ask someone's name after having a mindful conversation, it's either that the person extra oregano on your pizza or you are just a klutz.

We didn't have pizza at the wedding.

My day had started just normally.

I travelled more than half the way to the bank to deposit a check when I realised it was a second Saturdayand the bank must be closed. I had to turn back. I went back to my office because I wasn't as lucky as thosebankers who got an off on Saturdays too. Then I remembered I had to withdraw money from the ATM,which was obviously, as it's my destiny, near the bank.

The ATM was closed due to malfunctioning. I was so annoyed when my boss denied me to pay today'sfull salary as I had gone out of the office for more than one hour.

Worse still was when I had to pay for the coffee mug that broke. Now, no one ever in my vicinity, if not world, had the record of breaking sixteen coffee mugs in a week except me.

However, this one wasn't my fault.

I told the waitress and the manager that it was that devil with the mask of an innocent child who broke the empty cup with his paper plane. I know it's quite impossible to believe that a paper plane could knock off amug, but it so unbelievably did. It was at that moment the child decided to fly the plane. The plane didn't last for a second straight in the air.

I gave up.

So you get the idea of how a clumsy man's normal days are.

I don't know how the paper plane managed to knock off a coffee mug I still think was too heavy for me to lift while drinking my latte but that was the least of my worries. Serendipity is not really a thing in my life.

It's all a myth. I might overcome my clumsiness, and the universe would surely end tomorrow.

I had to attend a friend's wedding at night and my boss had cut half my pay already. Now, He can cut a day's worth of pay, I don't really care. So, I set off for home early.

"Are you planning to come to the party in this costume only?" I asked my wife. She gave me a stern look.

"I mean you can. You'll still add to the party's brilliance."

"Flattery is not going to work." She replied with a smile which gave away her next move. "I have nointention to attend a cake shower with a new dress on."

Well, she could have just said no.

As I reached the party, everyone politely moved away from me as if I had the plague. My friends greetedme from far away. I can't blame them, fifteen minutes into the party, I had tripped over three people, and adog. They said they were very sorry to invite the inept klutz.

A debonair albino man walked over to me. He probably didn't know me or was obviously stupid.

"Mr. Bense, Right?" He greeted me with a grin. So he did know me. But no comments, he looked ratherwise.

"Sure. I didn't know I was famous," I replied with an awkward smile.

"That you are." He laughed. "But you are unusually famous. I mean, don't take it wrong, people talkabout a good person who is nice and heart warming, fine, but as much as I have heard, they rarely talk aboutstaying away from that person as well."

I looked at him sincerely and said, "To answer your curiosity,"

"Concern." He corrected them with air quotes.

"Concern," I continued, "My friends would rather let you worry about me than bathing in something they

don't generally prefer." With that, my hand knocked off a glass of Curacao Mojito from the table as if toprove the point.

The waiters nearby apologised for letting me near the table. They didn't bother waiting for me to moveaway, afraid I would crash into everyone in the party, and moved the table instead. I smiled through the pain.

Sure they were more graceful compared to me but that didn't mean I had to like it. My companionwas biting his lips, in an attempt to stop himself from laughing, that was alright except he was looking at me. Icoloured. My expressions weren't masking my pain enough.

"You have some mock tail to add to the style of your suit. Do you prefer it that way?" The man asked,offering me a handkerchief which I took gratefully.

Good change of topic.

As I was just going to clean the stain, a piercing scream interrupted my state of peace. Apparently, the wedding ring had gone missing.

Bad change of topic.

"Do you want this back?" I asked my fellow companion.

“Not really, it’s not mine.” He replied. “A bald man gave me this when I was coming over to you.”

It was either that the bald man was at my wedding party when I had vomited all over the people below thestage (long story) or he was smart enough to learn from others.

I wish it was the first one.

“My whole life has been a ‘no serendipity’ moment,” I said. “I always wished though, that this doesn’taffect others.”

“You know, serendipity is not really something that happens.” He replied. “It is rather seen. You are theone person in this room who makes this party interesting. Even though it might not really be amazing toyou.”

I snorted, “But of course, I have better things to do than pitying myself.”

With that said, I kept the handkerchief in my coat pocket and moved over to my friend. He was perturbedand sweating. I have known him since we were in college. He got worried over small things.

“It’s okay, pal.” I kept a hand on his shoulder. “At least you didn’t step on your brides wedding dress andtore it.”

He laughed a bit. “Sure. You are still funny.” I took out the handkerchief and gave it to him. It was at thatmoment I knew that the word ‘ill-fated’ was made to address me, and the word 'fluke' was made to mock mebecause a shining diamond ring dropped from the handkerchief. I watched with stunned silence, anticipatingwhat was coming as my friend picked up the rolling ring, identifying it finally.

"It's impossible." My friend said, staring between the ring and me. "He can't do this."

"Yes!" I replied with a sense of relief and gratitude, "of course I can't." I thought I would be kicked out ofthe party after that but at least I was trusted by people.

"I wouldn't have allowed him near the rings either." The bridesmaid said. She didn't really have to saythat…

Now that finally my clumsiness and haplessness were helping me somewhere, it had to be this way. Butthe question was still, if not me, then who?

A few hours later, the CCTV was checked by the cops. As it turns out, the thief was the bald man whohad given my companion the handkerchief which ended up with me. The thief, if not for the excuse that hewas a kleptomaniac, would have ended up in jail.

"I guess you were right," I told my companion after the wedding was over. "Serendipity is not reallysomething that happens, it takes those beautiful eyes."

"I am Malcolm, by the way." He said starting with an awkward smile and then cracking up at the look onmy face. I'll surely remain gauche.

FROM THE DESK OF THE PRINCIPAL – MESSAGE TO THE AUDIENCE

'If a child cannot learn in the way we teach, we must teach in a way the child can learn.'

Delhi World Public School, Noida Extension has played a crucial role in shaping a child's future, not only by the provision of education and ensuring learning, but by molding the character, morals, and value system of the child too. Providing opportunities through various activities is a way to discover the children's latent talents and ensure their holistic development.

We believe that education is a synthesis of academic brilliance and creativity, and as the Principal of the school, my mission is to encourage and enable our students to develop as sound, introspective, and modest individuals with discerning minds, ready to make a difference in all aspects of life. Thus, through this holistic approach towards education, the school focuses on all aspects of a child's growth, not just their academic advancements, thereby establishing an overall wellbeing.

Children are often compared to clay, as they are pliable and can be molded into the shape we desire. With proper guidance and grooming, they have the potential to become exemplary individuals such as authors, entrepreneurs, leaders, and other multifaceted personalities. At DWPS, our mission is to cultivate ethical leaders and sportsmen whose signatures are sought after as autographs. To achieve this, we are committed to providing a stimulating learning environment that encourages self-analysis and exploration of each child's unique talents. Our ultimate goal is to enable our students to reach their fullest potential and blossom into successful, well-rounded individuals.

Our initiative of Joyful Learning has brought a sparkle in the eyes of students and through this amalgamation of learning and happiness, we have been successful in discovering our bright and budding authors, whose compositions have given us the encouragement to publish this collection of their pearls of wisdom. The publication of this book is indeed a moment of pride and excitement for the entire DWPS family and we believe that this endeavour is just a stepping stone that would lead us all to the threshold of world class stories, novel and poetry with a never ending chain of discovering new authors ready to conquer the world with the power of the pen.

Before concluding through this forum, I would not refrain from expressing my gratitude to the parent fraternity for entrusting to us their most cherished possession. I, on behalf of my institution, assure you our best efforts, always. We shall continue to surprise you with many such moments of pride in future.

With all my love, best wishes and blessings.

Ms. J. Arora
Principal

ANECDOTE PUBLISHING HOUSE – UNCUT STORY

Sagar Azad founded Anecdote Publishing House with the sole **purpose** of building a connection of the quality readers with the quality writers worldwide. Their **vision** is to let readers discover quality content across multiple literature consuming platforms – print, e-books & audio books. They provide authors with professional & intellectual guidance & creative support that they deserve to gainfully pursue their passion, and to make their work reach consumers of quality literature, worldwide.

They are envisioned to build an ecosystem of quality writers, editors, proofreaders & designers and give their readers an unparalleled experience of quality literature. On their mission to achieve their vision, they proudly espouse the **values** of encouragement, enablement, equality & quality.

Encourage everyone to spawn creativity: They believe that the reader is as creative as the writer. And everyone between the writer and the reader has their own creativity. The founder Sagar Azad deeply respects the creativity brought in by all professionals engaged in the journey of the work from the mind of the author to the hands of the reader and he strongly encourages it.

Enablement to reach readers: They are committed to ensuring that once they undertake a publishing work, they turn all the stones required to make the work reach its intended reader, thereby delivering happiness & satisfaction to both the readers and the writers.

Equality for & towards all: They treat all people equally no matter the gender, region, faith, nation.

Quality for all: With decades of experience in the book Publishing Industry, Sagar Azad is obsessed in providing quality literature to the readers, quality services to our authors, quality employment to his employees and quality relationship to his partners.

Anecdote Publishing House is headquartered in Delhi with its PR, marketing & distribution arm Champ Readers Private Limited.

ED INNOVA – UNCUT STORY

Founder **Dr. Susmita Gupta** founded Ed Innova with the sole purpose of providing quality writing services to all start-ups and individuals. In June 2021 she formed Ed Innova and Later in December 2021, she expanded the vertical of Ed Innova with the addition of PR services and other services that enhances the brand building of any business and individual personality. Now Dr. Susmita Gupta has taken the initiative to felicitate distinguished personalities, brands, and businesses of India. Her organization Ed Innova, believes in honoring the achievements of individuals from every field with a recognition award so that it motivates them and inspires others too to do a great job in their own field. It will not just acknowledge the individual's success but also recognize their ability, struggle, effort, and excellence above all.

Ed Innova has been felicitating distinguished brands, Personalities, and Businesses of India with Awards of Distinction and they are continuously honoring with a boost of morale for every distinguished brand, Personality, and Business.